Dr Ragab's Universal Language

Robert Twigger is the prize-winning author of several previous books, including *Angry White Pyjamas*, for which he received the Somerset Maugham and William Hill awards. He is married and lives most of the year in Cairo.

By the same author

Lost Oasis

Voyageur

Being a Man in the Lousy Modern World

The Extinction Club

Big Snake

Angry White Pyjamas

Dr Ragab's Universal Language

ROBERT TWIGGER

PICADOR

First published 2009 by Picador

First published in paperback 2010 by Picador
an imprint of Pan Macmillan, a division of Macmillan Publishers Limited
Pan Macmillan, 20 New Wharf Road, London N1 9RR
Basingstoke and Oxford
Associated companies throughout the world
www.panmacmillan.com

ISBN 978-0-330-42747-0

1 3 5 7 9 8 6 4 2

A CIP catalogue record for this book is available from
the British Library.

Printed in the UK by CPI Mackays, Chatham ME5 8TD

To Samia Hosny

Part One

Prolegomena to a Burial Alive

1

We live in the past. We live in the future. I wish (and don't you?) that we lived more in the present. It isn't very easy: we used to cower in caves; now we hunker in bunkers.

I should explain I have a thing about bunkers.

Helmut had a bunker. His family had a bunker. Helmut was the grandson of a German industrialist I was supposed to write about. The family bunker; in Germany. I was so excited. Just the thought of it made me want to visit.

Bunkerlove. As a child my parents favoured Padstow on the Cornish north coast for holidays. We alternated day trips to churches, tin mines and castles with visiting the beach. Sometimes we saw Cornish wrestling in the pouring rain. But the best days, which in my memory were always sunny and windy, were the beach days – either at Rock, Trevone, or, my favourite, St Georges Cove.

St Georges Cove had an ancient well, but much more importantly, a pillbox, that is, a one-roomed hexagonal fortified gun emplacement. A bunker. My first bunker. You had to go down a narrow flight of concrete steps. Inside it was dark, silent, and odiferous. A smell of urine and seaweed, that bubbly black seaweed you can pop. You didn't really want to walk about inside. Just stand still and imagine yourself in your own war movie.

Was there graffiti? I think so – though this was before the

widespread availability of spray cans. Maybe a swastika or two. In those days abandoned buildings always attracted swastikas, as did school desks and exercise books. Swastikas seem more generally reviled now. At the same time there has been no let up in their production – but not on desks and exercise books; now they are corporatized and capitalized into cable history-channel specials, camp memoirs both real and fake, endless 'new angles' on the Third Reich lavishly illustrated with famous flag moments shot by Leni Riefenstahl.

Anyway, not for me castles, dungeons and other such Robin Hood type attractions. For me the benchmark of romance, escapism, adventure was the pillbox. That was the beginning of it. Then I discovered air-raid shelters.

My great-aunt, who lived in Worthing, a resort favoured by retirees, had one. The old shelter was at the bottom of her garden. It had the magic narrow stairway leading to a dank interior, a store place for weedkiller, peat, plant food, flower pots. The only light was the dim glow from the sunken entrance. It was, in a way, a loathsome place, and yet I was strangely attracted to its earthy, musty smell; its myriad possibilities. I used to play there with a girl who lived across the road. Innocent stuff but already sex had wormed its way into the unstable cauldron of bunkerlove. Air-raid shelters became my new fixation.

I read about war. I envied people who had been in the Blitz. I learnt that lucky Rommel had a tunnel from his house to his own personal air-raid shelter. My father subscribed, for what seemed like years, to a weekly magazine that built into a six-volume Purnell's picture encyclopaedia of the twentieth century. I spent days staring at the awful mesmerizing images of two world wars and, incidentally, many pictures of bunkers.

I knew by then that pillboxes and air-raid shelters were a subset of my love of bunkers. Deep underground, away from the bombs, nuclear or otherwise, one could live at peace. I also loved *The Hobbit* and *Wind in the Willows* for similar and allied reasons.

Though it seems more significant now than it did then, part of my family's mythology was that my grandfather owed his life to a kind of bunker. He had been a POW in Japan and survived the nuclear bombing of Nagasaki by being down a salt mine. He emerged from his slave status as a salt-miner to discover Nagasaki utterly destroyed. Interestingly, despite witnessing the devastation at first hand he never forgave the Japanese for the tortures they had personally inflicted on him. He never bought a Sony product or a VW either come to think of it.

In our garden in the country I took to building earthen bunkers. I had a friend who joined me. We linked our bunkers with tunnels that sometimes collapsed. Even today the smell and feel of earth in my hair is more than nostalgia, it's what the Japanese call *natsukashi*, that intense bloom of feeling for times past that Proust's madeleine invoked.

In my late teens I was caught up in various attempts to spread world peace through writing letters to world leaders and going on demos. Showing support for the women protestors camped at an American airbase I caught my first glimpse of a truly huge bunker – the grass-covered concrete super bunkers used to house cruise missiles. These silent structures were like prehistoric long barrows, mini-hills with steel doors at either end, all neatly turfed with greensward.

The KGB were also involved, naturally. From defector documents such as the Mitrokin archive, it seems that the good-hearted old UK peace movement was actually infiltrated and controlled by the Soviets. Why? It was an attempt to stop us *building bunkers*. Unlike the Swiss, who had always been very pro-bunker, there was a strain of anti-bunker feeling in the British peace movement that I never really understood. The no-bunker-building idea, which we now know originated in cunning *sovprop*, was based on the premise that in a nuclear war we would all be dead anyway so why bother with bunkers? Bunkers would just give us a false sense of security and make us believe we could survive a nuclear attack. Therefore we should unilaterally disarm – which was what the Soviets wanted.

Years passed. My love of bunkers took a conversational turn. I learnt to disguise my passion with humour. It became a party piece. Then, about five years ago, I was rooting through a library chuck-out box when I found *Pillbox*, an unlikely (though utterly real, I assure you) coffee-table book that is the last word on . . . PILLBOXES, together with pictures, schematic diagrams and the six-figure Ordnance Survey coordinates for most of the five thousand pillboxes in Britain.

Pillbox locations were never recorded. Local Home Guard units simply memorized where they were. The idea was that, in an invasion, the resistance could occupy fortifications unknown to the Germans even if they captured Britain's defence plans. Even if the Nazis tortured Winston Churchill the pillbox secret would be safe. Then, in the 1970s, scattered groups of pillbox historians started to record data. This led to the immense project of listing for the first time the whereabouts of all the pillboxes in Britain. Pre-Internet, it was undertaken in the 1980s and early 90s by a number of enthusiasts who pooled their resources to run a twenty-four-hour 'pillbox hotline'. If you found an unlisted 'box' you could ring in and have it recorded.

I searched the list and saw that while St Georges Cove was listed, there was no mention of a pillbox I had visited one night as a teenager in 1981. This pillbox, one of many along the valley of the River Thames, was hidden by a large willow in the corner of a wheat field half a mile from any road. I had gone there with friends who had heard there was 'a party' happening. But the pill-box party was just four boys sipping cider staring glumly at a fire they had lit. You could see the flickering flames through the slit window from quite a distance. It didn't help that the lads were from a different, and therefore much reviled, school. I joined with my mates in roundly dismissing the budding beatniks and their choice of venue, the tiny number of guests, the fact that there were no girls there. As we left I even, to gain further credibility, threw a lighted banger through the window. It went off with a muffled thump and we retreated giggling and smirking to our muddy ten-speed bikes left in the corner of the field.

I include this pillbox encounter as an example of how you can in teenage years turn against that thing that is 'really you'. Only later, when I began that slow process of losing touch with teenage friends, could I see what a dastardly betrayal of the pillbox this attack had been. Or something. As an act of contrition I decided to not phone in the coordinates.

The thing that really caught my imagination, however, about *Pillbox* was the endpaper maps, which showed Britain criss-crossed with lines of pillboxes. These lines snaked across the country like a sinister variant of such anodyne routes as the Ridgeway, the Pennine Way, the Cornish Coastal Path.

A year or so ago, armed with *Pillbox* and a collection of

one-inch OS maps, I walked from Bristol to Croydon following the continuous line of fortifications across Southern England – perhaps the first-ever traverse of 'The Pillbox Way'. There was one every two miles or so, often hidden by blackberry bushes or high nettles. Part of the fun was being the first person to see the next one. I went with a friend, Jason, who, halfway, developed a curiously inflamed toe making further hiking with me impossible.

Jason had only a passing interest in pillboxes. Months later, when his toe had healed, he confided he had grown to 'hate and fucking loathe' them but had been too polite to mention it. The thing is I agreed. After poking my head into about fifteen a day, every day, I, too, had grown a bit sick of them. But that sickness was also part of the attraction. I couldn't stop thinking about them. The idea of their very existence filled me with a strange excitement.

It was their darkness, their permanence, and the metal bits stuck into the concrete. It was important that pillboxes included some metal. For these reasons I was also drawn to abandoned railways, especially abandoned tunnels, which yawned, dark and gaping, down a hillside hidden by dripping trees that had grown since the big railway closures of the 1960s. If I could find evidence of metal, tracks, metal securing pins, old signalling gear it was all the better. Metal, which strengthened concrete in any bunker, was the matrix of my warped desire. It was as if the transgression of the earth by our metallic intrusions signalled a new and dangerous direction, a siren's call I had to follow.

And so to Germany in a Peugeot 106.

2

I had been commissioned by a vanity publisher, one that occupied a fine line between vanity and reality (the author got paid but so did the publisher – by the client not the public). A large aluminium company based in Germany but with offices in Cleveland, Ohio and other such places wanted an updated English version of their company history. Company histories are intrinsically boring, they have to be, otherwise the company appears unreliable. German company histories, though, are allowed to show the far-off influence of *theory*, faintly but distinctly, theory and statistics. You might even get away with a touch of Spengler, a nod at Hegel and brush stroke or two of Husserl in a German company history as long as the bell curve, standard deviation, mean and median are all there. Naturally the English version needs then to be sanitized for people who think philosophy is something best left to Harry Potter. The English prefer what they call *real history*: dates, details, facts without speculation – that was my job. I had permission, and a meagre expense account, to go down to the firm's founder's family schloss to dig up the dirt. And then bury it again.

After a lot of phoning and faxing I discovered the schloss was really a farmhouse but they, the elderly grandchildren of the founder, did have an awful lot of family papers stored in a . . . get this . . . bunker. I knew then I would have to visit.

So there I was on a lovely spring morning pottering rather

than powering along the autobahn in my Peugeot 106. The sun was shining and all earlier anxiety had flown, the anxiety of locking up and leaving not helped by touch-and-go traffic down to the ferry port. But the sun shone and the anxiety melted, replaced by an almost absurd feeling of contentedness. Hour after hour I plunged southward through Germany riding the grey autobahns as they ribboned through forests and deep embankments. My vision of Germans and Germany was limited to the travellers' motels and chain eateries along the motorway where you had to speak German and they served very nice sausage stew. Then, on the second day, I finally left the autobahn and entered a beautiful countryside of small fields and wooded winding roads. For an hour and a half I drove through more and more rural areas until, with my faxed map upside down on the steering wheel, I made a left turn. There were fir trees on either side now, close packed right up to the single bar of wooden fencing, as if the fence was holding back a force of nature. The soil all around was sandy, you could see it at the sides of the unsurfaced road. I happily drove on, splashing through puddles. After two or three kilometres the road climbed a hill. I could see a great open 'V' of sky in front of me and it reminded me strongly of trips to the seaside as a child when you absolutely know the sea will appear beyond the next rise. And indeed, as I crested the hill, I saw a great stretch of water in front of me. Helmut, one of the grandchildren, had spoken of a lake in passing, as if it were just a big pond. But this was truly a small sea, an inland fjord with a rock at one end like a great tooth sticking up.

The house was large but not showy, rustic, inspired by log-barn architecture I thought, and spread around a courtyard. Everything was spick and span. The sawn logs were so neatly racked in the outhouse they looked unreal, like a magazine advertisement for the rural life.

The grandchild, Helmut, and his wife, Claudia, both in their sixties, came out to meet me with their two bounding retrievers. The grandson of Germany's greatest aluminium entrepreneur was short and thin. He was wearing shorts and white socks and Teva sandals and his legs had the goliath bulges of serious varicose veins. He was cheerful and friendly and of course he and his wife spoke good though slightly accented English. He had been an atomic scientist but now regretted it, apart from the way nuclear power reduced acid rain. He showed me the blotched oak leaves of a courtyard tree and shook his head. 'Acid rain, acid rain.' It was a little intense to be discussing the destruction of the planet before even entering their beautiful log home but I countered with a few examples of serious UK pollution such as Sellafield which was a bit silly as my own knowledge was transparently limited to knowing the place had once had a different name, i.e. Windscale. Inside, in their long low sitting room, one wall was covered in records and CDs, Pink Floyd mainly. Helmut's eyes lit up behind his serious square glasses as he tried to enlist me in his enthusiasm for *Dark Side of the Moon*.

Then Claudia, who had very short hair cut fashionably ragged, I felt, and bright red lipstick that contrasted with her leathery skin, asked me what kind of tea I would like. They were trying to be thoughtful. Their son, who worked as an aerospace engineer, had an obsession with tea. Though he no longer lived at home his extensive tea collection remained for when he visited. His parents had taken the interest upon themselves and probably thought an Englishman would appreciate the chance to drink honey and ginger tea mixed with a little lapsang souchong.

After a longish detour through the early history of rare metals, I asked, 'When can I see the bunker?'

Helmut's bespectacled round eyes looked surprised. 'Any time,' he said, 'though we can send someone down to bring up the papers you require.'

'There's no need,' I said, 'I kind of like bunkers.'

At dinner I drank deeply of their homemade cider and later of the distinctive apple brandy that was a speciality of the region. Now I became animated in my love of Pink Floyd, which, under the soothing influence of too much alcohol, struck me as highly original and audacious; indeed how could I have overlooked for so long such brilliant licks, lyrics and solos? Helmut seemed pleased by my enthusiasm though he did correct me on a few matters of rock minutiae. Claudia and 'the help', an attractive Czech woman in her thirties, with big forearms, did all the clearing away and then we all, including the 'help', had to listen to *The Wall*, which has always been my least favourite Floyd album. Helmut took off his glasses and massaged his eyebrows while at the same time nodding his bald, grey head to the beat.

I began to feel a growing disdain for the gentle grandson of Germany's greatest aluminium magnate, which may have been rooted in something primordial, but took the form of disgust at his reverence for Pink Floyd, a reverence only minutes before I had been stupidly encouraging. Here was a man, aged over sixty, who should know better, surely? Surely he should be into all that classical music that I, too, at some stage in the very near future planned to fully appreciate?

I slept badly and awoke feeling dehydrated. There was no glass to drink from and I had to greedily suck water from the tap. The view over the lake cheered me up. I saw what I thought was an eagle flying above the rock island at the far end.

Finally I got to the bunker.

I walked there after breakfast with Helmut, who was still in his sprightly shorts. We went along the grassy edge of the lake. Upside down was a corroded aluminium boat with long strands of grass growing around it, too close to the boat's sides for the lawn mower to cut. This was one of the many aluminium artefacts the founder had had made. In 1860 aluminium was worth more per gram than gold and silver. The founder even gave his wife an aluminium wedding ring (it left a blue mark but she never complained, apparently). He also had an aluminium bath tub. I was feeling athletic and buoyant, and I went to lift up the boat. 'Careful,' said the grandson, 'there are sometimes snakes, the vipers, under there.' I lifted the boat slowly but there were none.

A spit of woodland jutted out into the lake. We followed a pine-needly path that went through the woods. On the other side we broke free of the trees and came down to the lake. The sky was pure light blue. It was quite windy. Waves caught the light in tiny packets of brilliance before breaking on the gravel shore.

Away from the water the forest had been cleared into rough pastures. But as we approached I saw the overgrown remains of a house that had fallen, or been demolished. Creepers and grass grew over stumpy low thick walls. Blackened balks of timber lay crosswise on the ground wreathed in briars and bindweed.

'Big house,' I said.

'Used to be. It was built by my grandfather without using any nails.'

'Why?'

'He didn't like nails.'

Now that was weird, but I probably couldn't put it into the company history. Or maybe I could.

We went through the ruined house and nearby there was a raised area of lawn. I could feel the hairs rising and the back of my neck get cold with excitement – the unmistakable outline of a bunker. There was a low brick wall concealing concrete steps leading down about three metres. There was water at the bottom.

'Is it flooded?'

'I don't think so. Do you want to go down?'

I nodded, unwilling to speak.

Helmut had brought keys and two small plastic torches. (An Englishman would have been less well prepared, I felt.) I started to get the creepy feeling I always get around bunkers. The revulsion that I have to overcome. It's like the feeling of having to grow up a little. Or look at a wound you suspect is worse than it is.

I started down the steps and Helmut passed me down the key, which was attached to a small piece of red wood. The keys were strange, not like Yale keys, they had teeth sticking out at right angles in four directions.

There wasn't enough room for two on the narrow stairs. The water was just a puddle, stopped by a concrete lip below the door which was wooden, oak, grey with opened grain. I put the key in and it didn't work. When I pulled it out the key end was wet with rust-coloured water. I tried pushing the key further in and with a hard turn I opened the lock. The door juddered open.

More steps led further downward into darkness. This is a real bunker, I thought. A real deep bunker. I counted the steps as I went. There were twelve, all narrow and high. At the bottom was another door, less weathered looking, it looked as if someone had painted a rose on it. I kept flashing the torch on it from different angles but it was hard to see in that kind of light. I pushed the door and it wouldn't open. Helmut was right behind me now. I could sense that he too was somehow infected by bunkerfever.

'This key,' he reached over me and selected another key, there were three.

This key slid in and the lock clicked open easily. Ahead of me was a wooden wall that looked as if it was made from upright railway sleepers, yellowish in colour. Across them was daubed in dribbly red paint 'wilkommen zuhause' – like the painted messages you get in horror films.

'Have you ever been down here?' I whispered, for no reason.

'Many times – when I was a schoolchild.'

There were doorways – one on the left and one on the right. I shone the torch through the right doorway. The room was a wood-lined cube. Like a small attic except it was a cellar. A miniature Bjorn's cabin, if you've read *The Hobbit*. I went in and touched the ceiling and both walls – all wood except low down, set into one wall, were a row of circular holes, three lines of cobwebbed earthenware pipe ends. 'The wine store,' explained Helmut. All gone now.

The wooden floor was littered with old magazine pages, the 1950s kind where the colour has that powerful painterly tint to it. I reached down and picked up a page – it was a tattered picture of an American car, the paper quite dry. I was surprised. I flashed the torch up and around. The walls were planked vertically with square pillars in each corner. Solid beams across the roof. 'It's all oak,' whispered Helmut, knowing full well that you always whisper in bunkers. There was a musty smell, not damp, the smell you get when you stack old newsprint for too long in the sun.

'It's a bunker for one,' I quipped and Helmut nodded with his chin. 'The papers are stored over there.' A single three-foot-wide plank, like a wide shelf, maybe two inches or more thick, extended from the wall without support. It was rather stylish and I could see it had been a narrow bed. On it and under it were collapsing cardboard boxes of files half covered in a dust cloth.

'Actually this place was built by my uncle. He even sheltered someone down here during the war.' He nodded matter-of-factly. 'And he married her too. Afterwards.' He paused. 'A Jewish person.'

Forget aluminium. This was a real story. I could see my editor telling me to work it in as a footnote under comparative sales figures since 1940.

We poked around in the other room, which contained a wooden loo seat over a 'thunderbox', a hole that went down even deeper and even the torch did not reveal the bottom. There was a tiny aluminium (of course) sink with a single pipe and a tap. No water came out when I turned it.

Helmut coughed. 'There is some controversy now over aluminium in cooking utensils though nothing has been clinically proven.'

'Don't worry,' I said, improvising, 'my kettle is aluminium.'

Helmut said no more, assuming that I had been briefed to only mention the virtues of aluminium and not the fact that it caused Alzheimer's. There was a time when I would have been adamant that I mention all the latest anti-aluminium health-scare information but those days were long past. Now, whenever I hear the word controversial I reach for my red pen.

Helmut was happy talking about his bunker-building uncle. 'Yes, he was a real eccentric figure, very fond of travel. Also somewhat unlucky, he was in trouble with some brigands after the war here.'

'Brigands?'

'Yes, the armed gangs that roamed over Germany until 1947. Seeking revenge. Many were also Jews, but it is not so written about, naturally.'

Pink Floyd, Bavarian apple brandy, acid rain – my arse, *mein host* was a Nazi sympathizer, I could sense it. The kind who keep it hidden, half hidden.

'Up there,' he said flashing his torch upwards. I looked up and saw a square hole in the ceiling, blackened as if by fire. A kind of shaft. 'That leads to what used to be the old kitchen on the surface.'

'The emergency exit,' I said. All bunkers have an emergency exit (for ventilation purposes if nothing else) unless, of course, the builders intend them to be tombs.

We went back to the main bunker room and I peered into files which were hasped into stiff-backed folders. Some of the paper was stuck together. I became distracted in my search. I wasn't sure what I was looking for. It was silly trying to read things by torchlight. There was other junk, too: a wine crate full of perished tennis balls, a child's tricycle. 'What's that?' I asked, unearthing a kind of treadle machine. 'A jigsaw, we used to use it to cut out funny shapes when we were kids.'

I was conscious now of being underground in an unpleasant rather than interesting way. The low ceiling. The darkness. The fact that there might be roaches or rats. Not to mention the tons of oak, earth and concrete above waiting to collapse in on us. I was a connoisseur of such moments, which always end in me fleeing the bunker, hole, cavern – or at least being glad to get out.

'I don't think I can find much here,' I said. Helmut assumed a sinister will to power and said in a sneering voice, 'I already said so. But we will have the cartons brought up for you to examine.'

Back on the surface we squinted in the bright sunlight. Helmut was entirely equable again. Bunkers do things to people, I knew that already. He showed me, amid the grassed-over remains of the kitchen, a wet wooden trapdoor that covered the bunker's emergency shaft. Then he consulted his Suunto watch (the kind that tells you if you're having a heart attack or not) and announced it was time for a Pilsner.

The cartons came up after lunch (no wonder the 'help' had such muscular forearms). Going through them was a long, hopeless and grubby task not helped by almost all the documents being in Gothic script, which even for a German reader is a pain. I made quick, increasingly random, decisions about what to take with me. All I really needed, I told myself, as I always do when collapsing a grand project in the face of hard work, were little extras, titbits – the bulk of the company history would come from the German edition. After two hours of sorting and a bit of note-taking I told myself I had enough material. And I'd seen the bunker.

As I was leaving, Helmut disappeared for a long while to find some personal papers belonging to his uncle. But he returned red-faced and irritable and said it didn't matter. He would send them to me. Claudia then told me with a certain amount of hesitation she had written a story rather in the style (though this wasn't her aim at all it was just a happy coincidence she said) of the zillion-selling Brazilian, Paulo Coelho. She thought it might be publishable. I sensed about the only perk being a writer gets you: illusory power over people's dreams of literary success. I smiled. 'I'd be happy to read it.'

3

Rule one of the bunker: get strong doors, at least as strong as the bunker itself. Saddam Hussein's great weakness we are led to believe was his bunker doors, substandard, apparently, and subject to bunker-busters. His other failure was security – he allowed the plans of his bunker to reach the CIA via German intelligence sources who contacted the firm that actually built the bunker. Rule two of the bunker: always build your own, never, ever subcontract.

My flat in Ealing is one of many in a large red-brick family house that once must have been beautiful. It has one tiny bedroom and a larger room with a kitchen where you have to bend like a giant in a doll's house to tend the stove. Like many flats carved out of old houses mine has an odd feel – the ceilings are too high for its size, making the dimensions feel vaguely wrong. There are still the old plaster mouldings but they are only on three walls. The best thing is that I have a bay window that looks out over the off-road parking. My room, though nominally on the ground floor, is high above the level outside and impossible to climb up to the windows, which are double-glazed, extra-strong, in special frames etc.

One per cent of the cost of my London flat was the door. I put down the deposit, exchanged contracts, moved in and three days later I was burgled. They took nothing except an SLR camera with a flat battery, a video recorder, some silver cufflinks and a faded duvet cover which was used, presumably, as a swag bag. The worst thing was they kicked the door in, smashing both the lock and the frame. I found it strange that crime had reached a level of brutality where the physical surroundings were at risk. Burglars were no longer expert lock-pickers but desperate thugs good with the boot. I felt all the usual feelings of anger and impotence which the man at McCorquondales ('the difference between us and a locksmith is the difference between a Rolex and a Swatch') competently translated into a fat fee for his company. 'What you want, mate, is the "drug dealer". It's a joke, like, but that's what we call our steel door.'

He must have seen me coming because the moment he said it I knew I would have to have it. The natural hesitancy I had about indulging in bunker dreams now had a legitimate reason for being overruled – security. A steel door! With steel rods that slid into either side of the steel frame which was bonded to the walls with foot-long steel bolts. 'Your door's real weakness is not the lock but the hinges and the frame,' the amiable fitter explained, 'hence the need for cam-operated securing rods.' I looked at the diagram: they looked very reassuring.

The fitter said, 'You hear a bloody racket downstairs and what do you do? You make sure your own door is locked – you certainly don't go down and investigate.' The door was plated in metal that revealed itself in the minute hummocks of the rivet heads. Painted white it looked ordinary except for the three key holes evenly spaced down the right-hand side.

Everyone I told about the door was both keen and relieved. Everyone loved the idea of the steel rods running through the door, like the metal rods in concrete, the metal rods in bunkers. That door was worth every penny of the thousand pounds it cost me. A door fit for a bunker.

4

Today I received a package from Helmut. The envelope was padded. It was covered in German stamps. Inside were two bundles of papers. In the first bundle: about a hundred pages of fresh typing. In the second: a sheaf of yellowed newspaper clippings, mostly obituaries of luminaries in the Hertwig clan; a collection of older, yellowed, pages of typing; a handwritten manuscript to which was attached a Post-It note from Helmut explaining that this was 'a memoir of my Uncle Hertwig including his time in the prison bunker'. Then there was a photocopy of something that looked to be some kind of French and Arabic grammar book.

The hundred pages in bundle one were from Claudia. It would be nice to say Claudia was about to rival the wealthy Brazilian mystic Mr Coelho, but somehow I felt it was not to be. Even my good friend Cheryl, who is a fan of Paulo Coelho, would not, I think, be convinced. Claudia had penned a frankly unbelievable tale that centred around a faith healer in Heidelberg. Not that I didn't believe in faith healers, I did. It's just that when you write what you believe it comes out wrong, unbelievable actually. Belief really gets in the way. The easiest way to convince people is to write from the opposite point of view. Write what you don't believe. Be optimistic in life but never in literature. Not that I said this in so many words to Claudia. I put off writing back. Trampling other people's dreams into the dirt has never come easily to me.

I turned to the second bundle of papers.

Again I was initially disappointed. The first few pages of typing were a rambling account of the great aluminium dynasty founder by Hertwig senior, the grandfather of Helmut and the father of Martin Hertwig, the man who built the bunker. It was full of lists of the houses they owned and the people who visited their houses and the things they furnished their houses with. This was written by a family member identified solely by the initials H.A.H.

The photocopy was a French and Arabic manuscript printed in Bulacq, Cairo 1913, entitled: 'The Universal Language' by Dr A. Ragab. I scanned it (my French was adequate and mostly it was in French) and guessed that it was an attempt at an artificial language, like Esperanto, but using Semitic not Indo-European roots. There was a quote at the end by Haji Abdu Al-Yezdi, a poet I did not know:

> 'All is metaphor on this earth,
> As above so below,
> Of changed forms truth gives birth
> Visible like light to those who know.'

The rest of the bundle consisted of pages and pages of small neat handwriting written by Martin Hertwig. It started with some bare facts, rather awkwardly expressed. He explained he had loved his wife, the woman he had hidden; he had known Dr Ragab, who had taught him some kind of esoteric version of the Universal Language. He had been captured by 'gypsies and ex-convicts' and 'would have died . . .' Why would he have died? Several sentences were crossed out, and then the writing got smoother, smaller, faster. He underlined in capitals: 'I MADE

MYSELF INVISIBLE AND ESCAPED'. Then, 'Egypt 1961' and underneath it, 'Ignore the pathetic fallacy . . .'

It was as if he was making a fresh start to the story.

I had to go out so I bundled up the papers and took them with me. On the half-empty train into London I started to read.

Egypt 1961

Ignore the pathetic fallacy. Walls have ears. Mirrors have eyes. *Some mirrors.* Ceilings are like feet, some obviously unwashed. A door can be a giant ear too. The keyhole is the earhole. We live surrounded by all these things we pretend are dead, have never lived, are not living, seeing, feeling even breathing.

I write these words in sunny Cairo during miraculous times. Dr Ragab liked to ask: 'Would you recognize a golden age if you were living in it? How? By what means?' I suspect, sadly, it *is* a golden age, enlightenment forced on us by the squat spectre of the H-bomb. We know too much. We don't know enough. We forget that walls have ears and birds signal messages from other worlds.

I was in the cave, *the cave*, but this one was real, and I escaped. It wasn't all me – but then it never is. I had help from another dimension, the hummingly alive world of total darkness. A good place to start.

Part Two

Dr Ragab's Universal Language

1

The cave, or bunker, it was man-made, me-made in fact, was warm as toast and inside dark as burnt toast, the very dark brown of very burnt toast. Imagine you're in a dark room staring at a big piece of burnt toast two centimetres from your face. One centimetre. Black everywhere with a brown penumbra due to the curvature of the eyeball. Flashes of light like luminescent creatures in the super depths of the ocean. Retinal events. The moon half-glimpsed through the windscreen of a speeding car. Nights in the Orient.

I sat on the bunk edge and stared upwards for ages. Looking down I saw the same dark galaxy. The idea kept coming back to me: inner and outer are *the same*. For a few moments I persuaded myself I could tell the difference but I couldn't. In vain I looked for some shape but there was none, no depth, no surfaces, only the warm, toastlike dark. I shut my opened eyes, closed them, opened them; I felt the true vastness of the inner realm. Blind men live in this world. No wonder they were chosen as witchdoctors, shamans, prophets and seers.

The thought of Hagar up there, out there, Hagar with her luminous soul the other side of two locked and bolted doors. Not a sentence but then it's only half a thought.

Hagar was my light source, my life source. Hagar was a silly little girl. Hagar thought Hitler's dog was cute. Hagar had a strange upbringing amongst irresponsible adults that left her old-fashioned but imperturbable. I clung to one certainty: Hagar would never desert, leave, jump ship or bow out. When truth gets scratched out by confused numbskulls only loyalty remains. It's a dog's life, maybe, but don't be down on dogs, you can rebuild a world with loyalty.

There was much self-pity in that dark place, cured intermittently by fits of coughing. Interestingly I inhaled several cobwebs. They went down my throat like the last silvery integuments of a ghost. I believed in such things.

The cause of my suffering: a sorry squad of ex-prisoners of the Reich had locked me up in my own bunker. No doubt they had legitimate grievances. It may well have been, as Dr R often said, a punishment for a crime I was yet to commit. The conundrum was: was I there for a reason or was it a meaningless blunder on the part of fate?

My home had been invaded but instead of anger I felt fear. The kind of fear that has you scurrying down into your entrails and making up stories to support passivity. I feared for Hagar. I feared for her safety. Another part of me knew she could look after herself – the war was over. Then, I had hidden her from trouble in the bunker like a dog in a box, a kitten in a basket, a mouse in the hand – I hid her and her luminous soul from a world of wrong thoughts and unthinkable deeds. Now we had exchanged places.

Some facts about the bunker: the main room was 2.5

metres by 2.5 metres. The floor, roof joists and quoins and trusses were all yellow oak, monstrously thick, the finest *Quercus robur* you will find anywhere, though invisible now of course.

A small room on the left was also the 'kitchen' and privy. In a reprehensible act of desecration the armed assailants threw everything they didn't like down this dank hole thus blocking it with books, dried flowers, Hagar's drawings and then shat on it – or at least two of them did. I pointedly closed my nose to the brown stink. I hadn't the courage or desire to clear it.

The walls were made of planks twenty centimetres thick, hard as iron. There were no tools fit for digging – and beyond the oak there was rock and concrete. I built that bunker to withstand the apocalypse. I was buried and there was no way out.

The trapdoor. When I built the bunker I gave it a second exit. Mine went from the 'kitchen' area of the bunker up a five-metre vertical shaft to the scullery in the house. I should have installed a dumb waiter. Provided Hagar (and me) with room service. The rope ladder, attached to a ring in the wall at the top, had been pulled up.

With difficulty I 'chimneyed' up the shaft, back against one wall bracing bare feet against the other. At the top I hefted upwards with my head against the trapdoor – locked and bolted, it barely moved.

It's hard now to revisit that state of mind, even imprecisely. All comforting support had dropped away. My fingernails scraped against all kinds of thought as I fell, catching hold of nothing. Yet Hagar was up there, out there, sending me messages which I was too frantic to notice.

I knelt on the floor and hammered on the bunker door. At first normal hammering, as if I had been locked in by accident. Then I started booming on the door with a tight fist, knowing no one was listening. It became a kind of exercise. I crawled to Hagar's old shelf bunk in the darkness and lay waiting for something to happen. Hours went by and nothing. I had been buried alive.

2

It was Pascal who tried in vain 'to sit still in a quiet room'. I recalled with difficulty more favourite quotations. In special cases I think we become that which we read at the moment of reading, we become that author, who, in a real sense, lives again through us. Dr Ragab told me that when he studied intensely the ninth-century writer Junaid his handwriting changed. Once, visiting the darkened library vaults of Al-Azhar, he caught sight of an original letter by Junaid and saw the handwriting was very similar to his own changed style. He had become that man, or, rather, Junaid existed within him. Paying attention is the first kind of love – that which is loved, lives. Pascal sat in his chair and gave me the baleful look of a man long ignored. I took to groaning for amusement, a wan kind of entertainment akin to breaking wind. But even groaning can get tedious. I felt all around the edges of the bunker, discovering the row of hollow pipes that once contained wine. The bottles lay here, becobwebbed, for years, then, when the thugs saw them, they took the lot – three bottles under each arm, even that mediocre retsina I'd been avoiding for years, the one I was given by Bishop Montaine after his holiday in Salonika.

I felt new cobwebs, knocked into a watering can they

left down here with its roughened edge smelling of dirty coins, bumped my head on a roof truss – that gave me hope for some reason. I summoned up all the mental energy I could to match the darkness, but it soon dispersed. I was still falling, looking for certainties to cling to.

Eventually I slept. When I awoke I was strangely calm and alert, as if I had been washed up on the shore of a desert island. I blinked my eyes in the darkness. In the dark I miraculously heard the wind in the trees, even down there, beneath all that rock and concrete. My hearing, I thought, had always been acute, now I understood I had, in fact, been almost deaf, that there had been a huge blockage in my head allowing only the grossest, loudest noises to register. Now I heard everything. Super-acuity, always promised to the blind, had, indeed, befallen me. Sound scraped in tiny shoes across my huge eardrums. I heard the trees growing, pushing out roots, massaging the soft soil and licking up its moisture content. I heard the trees breathing in the wind.

3

The second day. Or perhaps the third. My body itched, perhaps bed lice or fleas, or more likely some kind of bodily reaction to being held in complete darkness. I wondered if I could last even another few hours in the darkness, like a blind white crab falling endlessly into the dark depths of the sea. I judged the days by the times that I fell asleep. They had stolen my automatic watch off my wrist with practised ease, sliding it off even as I fought back. The itch worsened.

Every so often I got myself behind the door and heaved. Nothing moved. Sometimes I used the back wall to get more leverage. The great door was jammed completely shut like the door of a wooden safe. I sat down on the bunk again. Something long forgotten made me search with my left hand, which is smaller than my right, down each wine slot at the side of the bunk. I was methodical, though I could see nothing. I found a small coin, a rubber band, an old nail and several detached wine labels.

The coin I fingered, trying to see the raised inscription in my mind's eye. The thin, crisp paper of a wine label I folded and felt the sharp edge. I made it smell of wine. My hands too. Hunger. Thirst. I sucked water from the tap in the privy's basin. Hunger caused headaches for a day. Then visions.

It was Dr Ragab who encouraged me to study the work of the ex-monk Giordano Bruno, who was incarcerated in 1592 under the orders of the Inquisition. Bruno wrote, 'You must make an enemy of time in prison. You must not wait for time to pass, instead resent its passing as you fill your days with worthwhile tasks, inner tasks.'

Time passes yet we cannot *imagine* time passing. I can visualize a pig or a rose. I cannot imagine the scent of a rose. I don't want to imagine the scent of a pig, though given the unsanitary conditions down here it might actually be easier. And by trying not to imagine something we often succeed. I think I can imagine a sound. I can hear music in my head. Beethoven. Gounod. Meyerbeer for some reason.

Bruno died in a cell inventing more and more complex ways of remembering things. He placed each memory in its own locus, one of nine that comprised an atrium, a memory room. There were twenty-four such atria that made up the memory house. To complete this system there were fifteen fields surrounding the house, each divided nine ways.

One of Bruno's many rules: no memory locus should be higher or wider than a man can reach. I can touch the ceiling; if I lie down my toes can touch one wall and my fingers the other. Perhaps I only exist as a memory in someone else's memory system. Whose? God's? Dr Ragab's?

Memory and dreams become dominant in the darkness. The usual significance of the outer world is reduced – but slowly, bit by bit, so you don't notice the change.

Lengthy memories that arrive unbidden, or seemingly unbidden, function like 'news' in the outer world. You feel in touch with something. They provide useful information, even entertainment.

The tooth I broke struggling with the thugs has left a taste of blood in my mouth. That made me think of two things – my father and what he called 'the day-dreaming of fools'. As a child I would sit for hours on my bed motionless, not even thinking except in a desultory associative way. My father hated it. He was a man of action and activity, fully there, so to speak – his dislike of the past meant he rarely talked of his own. I recalled him cutting himself whilst working and sucking the blood from the wound and spitting red froth onto the ground, several times, sucking his own wound clear. Then he would wrap the cut in a twist of sharp bladed grass and keep working. It was always nothing and my mother had long ago learnt never to enquire. My father cut himself with stolid regularity, as if he had too much blood flowing inside him, so much so that it demanded to be spilt on the dry earth. After such a cut, whether with the scythe, the sickle, his unsprung calf's-foot knife, sharp as a razor, or, most horribly, when he chomped into the web of flesh between thumb and finger with a pair of chicken shears, after such a cut my father, with sweat on his forehead and at the end of his nose, a cloudy salty drop of it, he always sweated even on frosty days, would stare at the cut as if he was proud and interested that he had yet again cut himself.

I have fainted before now at the sight and taste of my own blood.

I thought, on a rotating basis for hours, about scraping with the coin through the wood ceiling and digging up through the earth, but, each time before starting I remembered the rocks welded together with concrete. Two metres of it above me and then six of earth. I would need a pickaxe to get out that way.

The itching of my body grew worse. My skin, the largest organ of the body or so we are told, urged me to tear it off in a bloody strip from scalp to behind. I was wearing only a white shirt, undershirt, old corduroy trousers though I was warm enough. The bunker was always warm. I felt my undershirt was a friend, it was loyal to me however filthy it became. The itching was worst on the backs of my calves and the front of my forearms.

I lay down for longer and longer periods on Hagar's bed. It felt as if I was resting on Odin's wooden hand passing unbidden through the pillared wall. Sleeping and dreaming ran into different states of wakefulness. I saw, with a burgeoning detached interest, that the usual two states – awake, opposed to, and in contradistinction with, asleep, was, perhaps, wrong. Instead there were at least four states on a continuum, each more awake than the last, but certainly no absolute distinctions. Time passes differently depending on which state you are in. Dr Ragab said there is a trick to stopping time, really stopping time, but you have to teach it to yourself. Everyone's method is similar but slightly different.

I thought long and hard about what I studied in the East. How to send a message by thinking with your heart.

How to move an object by one's 'inner light'. All complete rubbish, of course.

I awoke on the third or perhaps fourth day to the sound of my sister calling to me from beyond the door. I was actually annoyed. I wanted to escape without help. The harder I listened the quieter her voice became. I had to pretend I wasn't really listening to hear her words, but still they were jumbled and, I detected, sentimental. My sister had been dead for eight years.

4

A scraping noise of inordinate magnitude became a rattle of bolts. This was no dream. Hearing footfalls on the trapdoor above I knew instantly who was who. Mr Particular was decisive yet hesitant on his feet. Oddsocks (all I'd seen of him, or noticed in the fight, was his one red and one green sock) had a sloppy tread with a slight shuffle. Roy gave nothing away, a neutral footfall which is neither fast nor slow. His was the only name I knew because it was the only name I'd heard used: 'Roy'll do this, Roy'll do that.'

I moved fast, half crouched already in subterranean adaption like one of H. G. Wells' Morlocks, to look up the shaft – source of the sound. Dirt fell into my eyes from nowhere. Then the trapdoor. I shielded my eyes. A face in black outlined against blinding light.

Everything dramatic is ludicrous in hindsight. Anyway *that* face, *the face of incarceration* (it was in shadow, but the sharp chin told me it was Mr Particular), regarded me for some seconds, saying nothing, and then he dropped the trapdoor with a tremendous bang.

First thought – Hagar must have revealed something, which is why they want me alive. Second: They meant to keep me here. Third: Ransom. Fourth: Revenge.

No food, no water, but I am still alive. I know they have

changed their minds. They meant to bury me. Now they have other plans. And so should I.

One thing has always fascinated me. That is: how does the dream, the imagined, the unreal, the words, the merest notion become real, experienced, felt, actual, a part of the world?

Long ago I learnt the theory of invisibility. In the bunker I began to think it might work in practice. I knew I was skating on thin ice. I had to ignore all protest from my rational self which told me the idea was absurd. But another side of me, the fanatic, maybe, was secretly pleased. There was no excuse to be 'reasonable' any longer – I now had in abundance what I never had before. Necessity.

What was the last thing Dr Ragab said to me?

'A man on a straight path never lost his way.'

5

The first food I suspected of poison. I ate a pinhead of potato, licked a fishbone. The smell of the tiny pieces of bony fish lasted on my fingers for hours. A day later, ravenous, I ate the lot. Greed is a great cure for fear.

They lowered things in a rusty fishkettle, an old one that had been left outside for years. Inside the kettle the food lay in a battered aluminium bowl. Black bread; watery soups; spicy sauces, cabbage leaves, fish from the lake but far from fresh, fried black and left long. They kept open the trapdoor as I ate, as if checking up on me. Like farmers watching a turkey fattening up on scraps. Why not cannibalism? I'd heard of such things in the camps. It all confirmed my instinct. When I had recalled the method I'd wait for my chance. When I was good and ready I'd be ready for when they opened the trapdoor. I imagined my arms twice their length reaching up and grabbing those pale greasy-skinned fiends.

They told me to shit in the galvanized watering can. It was the watering can I used years ago for the plants in pots on the terrace facing the lake. So far I hadn't. I couldn't. I was all bunged up. I'd pissed quite a few times but it must have been five days since I last shat. Partly, too, it was the size of the aperture – that and its propensity to unbalance.

If I wasn't careful there could be a nasty accident. The thought worried me less and less each day.

I had the bunker partly converted when Hagar was here – a mirror, a chest of drawers chocked up on one leg – in all the rush and confusion of those times that seemed a measure of my seriousness, my humanity. It still did, in fact. Snapshot snapshit. Groan. I turned over on the plank bed and examined the spiders. I now had a light, you see.

When my captors first imprisoned me they must have put something over the trapdoor that covered the crack around its edge. Now they were feeding me they still shut the trapdoor but left it uncovered.

My idea came from Egypt. Something Hagar never mentioned (typical!). The sun passed overhead and shone directly through the skylight in the scullery and down through the trap. The cracks let the light through. A single beam of light, which stretched from the sun, through the skylight, through the crack at the door's edge (indented by the hinges) and into my cave-prison as a solid bar of light illuminating the hurrying dust. My 'day' was, I calculated from the arc traversed, exactly two hours. My dawn came instantaneously and I never knew when. Twilight lasted longer, I'm not sure why, the light fading completely from fully bright to zero in about five minutes.

This wedge of moving daylight was concentrated in the area at the foot of the trapdoor shaft like a spotlight. The rest of the bunker remained dark and gloomy. I needed to spread the light.

In ancient Egypt tombs and pyramids are not lamp-blackened except by later explorers. So what did the ancients use as light? Polished bronze mirrors; angled down shafts shining the sun deep into the bottom of it all. I took up this idea, my first useful one, and placed Hagar's mirror at the shaft's foot, angled into my small prison yard. Light came weakly but it was enough to make the cobwebs shine, the oak glow.

6

The exquisite boredom of the condemned: unlike the ordinary prisoner, the condemned wishes for time to stretch on infinitely. He prefers infinite boredom to death. I wanted time to pass and I didn't want time to pass.

To measure my boredom I made a clock. (Dr Ragab always advised keeping busy.) From the blocked privy I retrieved two empty cans Hagar had used to hold pencils. I cleaned them and using my steel-heeled shoe as a hammer punctured one in its base with the nail I found in the wine-bottle pipe. Just the suspicion of a ragged hole, the merest break in the tin. I filled it with water and watched it drip into the other can. I started it at first light judged by the sun through the slit in the trapdoor. By the next 'dawn' the jar had overflowed. To slow the flow I folded flat one of the rough metal petals flowering from the microscopic drip hole. The next day half a can dripped through exactly. I measured it with a sliver of wood and scraped an accurate scale, inordinately pleased to have my hours back and even my half-hours!

My sense of smell was changing. For new odours it became as sharp as my hearing. But for the dull stink of myself and the bunker I registered nothing unless I sniffed hard. I smelt the dull almost sour smell of the seasoned oak and the smell of the earth around me, as piquant as seafood freshly caught, but perhaps that was just imagination. Sometimes, down the shaft, came the lingering evidence of Oddsocks' smelly feet in his broken-down shoes.

It was Roy that I feared, however. When they got me down here he lined up a punch and hit me squarely on the nose, not once, but twice in succession. The fight went right out of me. It was humiliating – all the blood and my eyes streaming with tears. But he just stood there waiting to unleash another punch.

All direction came from Mr Particular. Everything was his idea. He had authority but not an unyielding grip on the others. I suspected he rarely slept or slept very badly. Oddsocks I imagined was always on the brink of leaving but couldn't be bothered. Roy held them all together. I knew that Roy could do things that were real in their world – such as killing people.

Sometimes when they opened the trapdoor I could hear them upstairs breaking the necks off bottles and toasting each other. Strangely I only had curiosity not anger as I imagined my favourite vintages being slugged back by men who would be just as happy with potato liquor. There was no complaint about the retsina.

Roy and Mr Particular, apart from the number tattoo on his arm which I saw when they first approached the house, showed no evidence of imprisonment or even mistreatment. Oddsocks had some horrible scars, tears in his flesh bunged up with clammy white, on both his ankles. One of his hands had crooked fingers. I suspected he must have been beaten on the hand and had several fingers broken.

Enough about *them*, I'm writing this for a purpose, not to aggrandize my captors.

To become invisible I had to recall what I had mostly forgotten. The bare bones of the method. The magic (if you like) language expounded by my teacher Dr Ragab. I had to recall what I had once learned, half learned, learned enough – the secret letters and phrases of the Universal Language.

And then all I needed was the courage to practise it.

I was hooked, but instead of reading on, I grew excited at the thought of what might be inside the photocopy of Dr Ragab's Universal Language manual. I wanted to cut to the chase. I went by Tube to Notting Hill – the Central Line – I always try and avoid the District Line if I can. (I don't even like the green colour of the line.) In Waterstone's I bought a Hans Wehr Arabic dictionary (also a disagreeable green colour) to help me translate the photocopy. The French was not difficult and, flicking through, the only Arabic seemed to be words and short phrases. In the Arabic dictionary I first checked something that Dr Ragab mentioned in the introduction. He states that Arabic bears evidence of having been a 'created' artificial language. This revolved around the clusters of words associated with each three-consonant root. Depending on the order of the letters in the root and the vowels you inserted between them you change the meaning. And all the meanings relate to each other to reveal a subtextual concept, a kind of moral substructure to the language.

At random I found LZM which could become such words as lazim, lazma, luzum, ilzami and many more. The meanings ranged from 'to cling to', 'obligatory', 'necessity', 'duty', 'inseparable', 'to keep silent', 'to attend to', 'to display sustained activity', 'to persevere', 'to be attached or devoted to each other', 'zeal', and maybe a bit oddly, but maybe not, 'biscuit for the voyage'.

Ragab claims that words lose their meanings over time, but that Arabic was more resilient because of this conceptual underpinning. The words were a bulk definition of something unnamed. In the case of LZM it was a kind of extended notion of commitment with conscience.

After this explanation came a sentence that held my attention. DO NOT ATTEMPT TO LEARN THE UNIVERSAL LANGUAGE WITHOUT A TEACHER. Why? Obviously I ignored that.

Dr Ragab maintains that his Universal Language is not Arabic, but is related, an attempt to take the concepts in Arabic a step further so that non-Arabic speakers can partake of these buried ideas. But as I studied his language book I grew confused. None of his letters were the same as those in the Ham Wehr dictionary. There was a pronunciation guide but it also described postures to be adopted when speaking. Instead of A, B, C the letters of the Universal Alphabet were transcribed as short words, in roman letters as aluuf, beatt, geem, deem and so on. Then there were charts containing longer words but with brief, one- or two-word definitions: shemell means loquaciousness, apparently, fordung – overcoming. Without knowing the context, and why these words rather than others were important, it seemed somewhat pointless.

I went back to the memoir and picked up again at the point where Hertwig began to explain the Universal Language in detail.

7

I breathed out in the darkness the first letter.

Aluuf.

Strange how you never forget the first letter of a new language, the first number, the first words. Knowing this we should constantly be reversing the way we learn. Put the last first and the first last.

Aluuf.

To practise the Universal Language you have to be really *here*; present, not elsewhere, not dreaming about the future or thinking of the past.

The pronunciation was everything. Almost everything. The pronunciation displays the attitude, the inner stance of the speaker, how *here* they are, how present, how aware. With incorrect pronunciation nothing happened, and remembering is made harder. With the right pronunciation it was as if one were acting a role whose lines one already knew.

Take *Aluuf*. This letter was all in the final 'f'. The final 'f' had to have no destination. If one was focused without the inner tension of *desiring*, the 'f' extended smoothly and beautifully like something thrown. If one was knotted with greed for results, the 'f' stuttered out like a golfer striking continually at the ground and missing the ball. One must either be without the sort of desire that creates such tension, or one must learn some method of reducing it.

Luminous souls are born lucky in some respects – they just do not have this greed, this excessive desire for gain. (One knows it's excessive by how one reacts when desire is thwarted. A luminous soul can work hard in the pursuit of gain, but if thwarted, can walk away without a regret.) I was never like that, and my years away from Dr Ragab were wasted years in this respect. The only technique I knew to combat this greed was self-observation without self-judgement. But though that is the best technique when living a balanced and ordinary life, mine was far from balanced and ordinary; I was imprisoned in the bunker. I needed a shortcut.

There was only one: pain. Shortcuts are always tough in the Universal Language, very tough.

After leaving Dr Ragab I had fallen back on my old ways and become again a 'clever' person, and clever people hate pain. Because thought is effortless clever people assume that life should require no effort, exact no pain. If life begins to make demands it must mean the onset of some kind of stupidity. It is essential to be rid of this stupidity as soon as possible.

Clever people reveal themselves in their addiction to the effortless: drugs, sex, alcohol, food. Drugs are attractive to clever people because of their purity. There is nothing cleverer than a man in the grip of morphine addiction.

If they start to favour things that require effort – exercise, playing a musical instrument, work – they begin to undermine their own cleverness. The centre shifts.

The Universal Language attracts clever people and then gets them doing things they didn't plan on doing, such as physical exertion, manual labour, fasting, going without sleep. When the centre shifts they awaken to the shortcomings of cleverness. But not permanently. Everything can slide back. I knew that.

Each letter came with a posture. *Aluuf* is with the arms outstretched, fingers imagined as if elongated, stretched out ten, twenty, thirty metres. Stand as if crucified and stretch. Say the word. And again.

Another method of accruing calm, the kind of calm that negates this greed for results is to do good works secretly, without hope of reward, or even self-regard. Because one does not 'consume' one's good works a kind of calm space develops inside which is the antithesis of greed. This is the origin of charity – now debased into a way of gaining a reputation for being 'good'.

I may have performed a few good deeds in my life but certainly not many. I had rarely given time or money to anything charitable and only once or twice in secret. Like most people my main efforts, once I left Ragab, were devoted to self-advancement.

It was too late to be regretful, to realize one had failed to accumulate something as subtle as fairy dust. There in the bunker I had one luxury: I could be brutally realistic.

Which brings me back to the shortcut; the fastest way to make the Universal Language work was through pain.

What the ancients were fond of calling suffering, but pain gets to the point better and without the self-righteous overtones.

I tried an experiment. I wound my finger around a hair and gripped it tightly. But I couldn't bring myself to pull it out. I had become so soft.

Pulling out a hair was nothing. It was the lowest level of real pain I could imagine. But it would still hurt. Even the smallest pain still hurts. You can't cheat and have pain's benefits without the hurt. This is the utility of pain and its most important quality: there is no way around it.

I gritted my teeth and thought determined thoughts. I selected a new hair, this time a longish one growing from the swirl on my crown. I yanked hard and failed. The hair was stronger than me! I slapped my face with both hands, one then the other. With a harsh grab I jerked down, tearing out the follicle. Pain like that is always less than you imagined. Far less. And did greed desist or did I imagine it? *Aluuf.* The word resonated to my fingertips and back again.

Next, *be-att*. To be honest I was once skilled at doing these letters. I used to practise them for hours in the eight-sided study room on Dr Ragab's island. But the moment you think such a thought you can no longer pronounce them. Because you are no longer present. Because the self-congratulation is a desire for reassurance about one's ultimate success – in other words greed. That's how the Universal Language works. It can never be abused. It protects itself. And the strange movements and postures and visualizations are all designed to keep you present, because false imagining always happens when you aren't; everything comes back to that.

Be-att is in the 'B'. Wait for the right moment before roundly pronouncing it, like a man sighting a rifle and waiting, as the barrel wavers, for the precise alignment between crosshair and target. The movement for this one helps – head cocked right back whilst kneeling, Adam's apple pointing at the heavens. It's hard to say anything in such a posture, the 'B' always sounds like a croak at first.

Neem.

An easier one. Snap your fingers as you say it. If your mind remains clear you were 'present'. If other thoughts crowded in, then you were not. But one should beware of 'willing away' unbidden thoughts. It doesn't work. The right thing is just to observe them.

8

The exact ages of my captors were hard to tell. Because I was in their power they seemed older than I, despite their mistakes. They were undecided, they changed their minds. Mentally unstable, almost certainly. Bizarrely they appeared too polite to be able to carry out a murder. I knew, though, how it would happen. By stages. They'd beat me up verbally and then start the kicking. Get themselves into a frenzy. Hain was killed, after all. Different circumstances but the same outcome.

Hain had a wife who adored him and ten (ten!) children. He was a professor of archaeology with very good connections around the top men in the party, but fatefully he had the same name as an 'enemy' of the nation, a left-wing journalist then living in America. Poor old Hain. Thugs burst into his house on the night the militias were purged and asked that he accompany them downstairs to sign a legal document. (It always starts with some polite ruse or other.) After insulting and hitting him, they shot and killed him in front of his own fireplace. An hour later two more men came and forcibly removed the body for 'evidence'. Weeks later, when the mistake was discovered, an official apology was made to Mrs Hain and her husband's ashes returned, perhaps to stand on the mantelpiece above the very hearth where he was killed.

I knew all this because his wife sent me a stiff envelope lined with shiny black crêpe paper; inside was a quantity of loose powder. Not ashes but crushed bone. She sent envelopes with some of his remains in to all members of the faculty, all members who remained after 1934.

To be on the losing side in a major war is to be guilty of the only crime history cares about: losing. History is a tale told by the victors and the losers have to huddle in the shadows, blocked from the firelight. But I had long ago lost faith in the public project of 'history'; from Dr Ragab I had learnt that, in its desire for objectivity, history undoes its only virtue, its evidence of the cyclical nature of things. As facts multiply, history loses its usefulness as a guard against short-sighted thinking. And, according to Dr Ragab, the historicizing impulse is really a worldly projection of our own quest for a beginning, an answer to the question of who we are. When we lose sight of this, history becomes irrelevant.

During the war I suspected, no, I knew what was happening but did nothing, found nothing out. I told myself I was as much at risk as the victims in the camps. That's how you think when you live under a corrupt regime. You feel you cannot accrue guilt by simply living there. Doing nothing, you tell yourself, is not a crime. Doing what others tell you to do is a crime: Germany did not make war on the world by doing nothing; people did as they were asked to do. What did I do? I once gave a speech on the triumph of the light religions over the chthonic gods to a youth group interested in such stuff. As for refusing to teach 'non-denominationals' (Jews, of course), I actually kept all my students and then arranged a swap – giving tuition to another teacher's students in return for him teaching mine. This way a student could be registered as officially discharged but still be taught. This is how I met Hagar again after so many years.

I broke off reading and settled back on the stubby half-seat at the end of a crowded carriage on the Central Line. The London Underground is the biggest bunker complex in the world. It has secret passages, hidden stops, unused tunnels and even an entire old station left abandoned above the current Oxford Street station, which lies at a deeper level underground. The old place is still decorated with 1940s posters – untouched since it was last used and only open to staff (I got this from a magazine I subscribe to called *After the Battle*, the 'Blitz' edition). If you ever feel you're being watched at Oxford Street, you probably are – by the staff looking down.

I changed trains at Holborn, where it was windy. I love the strange winds that come from nowhere in the Underground and trap crisp packets against the wire-netting sides of the lift shaft. Weirdly, I felt at home here. I looked around at the unfamiliar, familiar faces, some friendly, some blank, some in a Tube trance, newspaper readers, backpacking tourists deep in a pocket *A–Z*, one outstandingly good-looking girl looking down and away, a man with too many tattoos.

In my past experience the present is, sadly, prosaic even when poetic – it never violates space-time, whatever that is. None of my Tube companions, my fellow travellers, is going to teleport to another dimension. I used to value the secure feeling of slamming a door shut on the miraculous. It seems like the logical act of an easily frightened man.

I continued reading.

9

Abiyat.

I imagined the trees outside in the darkness, the great branches moving in the wind. I said the first word. I should have waited but I didn't.

Abiyat.

Abiyat provides protection against psychic attack, a precondition to being felled by evil hands. Like all words it needs a mental image. As you speak you imagine yourself encased in a glass pyramid, perfectly transparent. It is one of the easier words, a test.

I understood that only through being invisible would I escape. I needed to increase the detail of my imagination to make this possible. The rest of the plan was simple: I would refuse to answer when they let down the food. Someone would investigate. I would be unseen, and, unseen, I would slip away.

I could not keep the image steady. The pyramid kept slipping out of shape. Perhaps I was distracted by the malignant thoughts of my captors. I started to doubt and disbelieve. The reality I needed to create was beyond me. I was getting ahead of myself. Certainly I had not practised enough letters. 'The alphabet keeps you honest,' said Dr

Ragab, 'every time you think you know something go back to the alphabet.'

Just for the heck of it I practised saying Abiyat a few times. I imagined the glass pyramid. It didn't seem so hard.

I spoke the first letter, Aluuf, stretching out the 'f'.

In my tiny flat in Ealing, unobserved, I did the stretch and said the word. Again and again. In a world of stymied motion, barred entrances, blocked exits, it promised action of a different sort. But then I began to feel very weird inside. Nauseous, actually. What was happening?

'To practise the Universal Language you have to be really here, present, not elsewhere, not dreaming about the future or thinking of the past. People who do that naturally we call Luminous Souls.'

I realized I was probably not a luminous soul.

10

Recalling the Universal Language, I found other memories came back to me. I thought a lot about the path that took me to Dr Ragab, how it had started with my father. I should probably explain about that.

My first memory of him: I was four, the great high quartered window of the nursery shining in the morning sun, my father there, holding up pyjamas to the light, my brother's, checking for semen stains. I was bewildered but he explained everything; the mood light-hearted, encouraging, scientific, curious not censorious, checking for nocturnal emissions part of the great adventure of discovery, learning, progress for all. My father was that most old-fashioned of beasts: a modern. He had a devouring interest in everything new, experimental, technical, mechanical – his great head, wide bald pate and dark-rimmed eyes shining like anthracite at the bottom of a deep mine. He was a checker, a trimmer, an adviser, a lecturer, a mother and a father, even though we had a perfectly good mother, he checked our stools before flushing, our teeth before brushing, our ears for wax our noses for snot, our necks for boils and our ideas for signs of religious sympathy. My father was a pure disbeliever, the Good Book (of which he knew a great deal by heart) sneered at, faulted, blamed, banned from our house, punishable by three days of not being talked to if you were caught with a copy. He did not beat us; he chose the more deadly and powerful tool of pretending you did not exist.

The texts he read aloud from on Sundays were Huxley, Bentham, Mill, Chamberlain, Saint-Simon, Compte, Ernst Mach and Hume's elegant disproof of miracles. Nietzsche was deemed 'unhinged' – my father preferred the dull cleverness of English philosophers, all dismantling religion word by word yet keeping quiet about their real beliefs.

He had a profound and unshakeable confidence in the latest research. For him it was a crime not to consult the leading authority, the most recent work. That was enough. As long as the right authority was followed, whatever the result, he was never tormented by the thought that he might have done the wrong thing. He did not believe there was any knowledge out there superior to what had just been discovered. 'Let us experiment!' was his favourite phrase, his clarion call, the source of a vital turbulent energy that drove all in front of him. Nothing was sacred (how he hated that word!), nothing was sacrosanct, all could be questioned, all could be improved – that was the tacit assumption, that the past was a blundering preamble to a glorious future. Not only was the baby thrown out with the bathwater, the bath was thrown out as well.

Beneath the aridity, though admitted solidity, of all this energetic questioning lay something disturbing. Dr Ragab told me (what later geological surveys confirmed) that the entire Egyptian Sahara rests on an underground lake some thousand metres down – the Nubian aquifer. The desert rests on water. This image stayed with me and thinking of my father it mirrored his strange relationship to ignorance. Beneath the surface loomed a vast pool of ignorance my father could never entirely ignore. It made him shake with fear. He could never outmanoeuvre it. This pool, this lake, of the great unknown, the unknowable, the never to be known, the impossible to even guess. His frantic efforts only revealed more of this huge unfathomable lake and as he grew older and his energy waned he put more and more effort into denying its existence by following systems, rat runs, tried and tested methods.

He never admitted his obvious fears. His fear of ignorance was my discovery. His fear of water was known to the family but not discussed. It was rooted in what he called 'a marvellous superstition'. A great-aunt, blind and considered (by the family elders) wise, had prophesied in 1861 that my father would die by drowning and as a result he had never been encouraged or even allowed to learn to swim. In early manhood he rebelled and became an excellent diver, though he remained a poor swimmer. Diving satisfied his desire, which was great, for attention; and it meant he did not have to remain long in the water.

'Not yet, not yet, wait until it is properly frozen!' In winter my father's fear turned into a horror of the lake's thin ice, the real rather than the metaphorical lake, that is. Skating on it. Falling through it. As the season grew colder he would watch as we hurled rocks onto the black ice dusted with white snow. Immobile he'd stand behind the curtains, his great helmet-like head, with deep-set eyes peering from the mullioned windows of the lake house. He would keep the window open, listening for the creak and boom of breaking ice. Around the jetty and small gravel beach the lake was littered with rocks of varying sizes, like a frozen Japanese garden. Each year we had to go further afield to find large enough stones which we rolled onto the ice, rocks big enough to finally convince my father the lake was safe for skating.

And then there was his magic. He would make a shiny penny appear from nowhere inside my stiff collar, or from my hair. Of course it was just basic palming but I remained utterly mystified for years, or so it seems now. My father had the one vital gift of the magician – he never explained. His tricks always retained the excitement of real magic – even later when I half guessed what he was doing.

If we went on holiday – always to rocky Bornholm in the Baltic – my father would make a show of packing his 'magic suitcase'. Whatever he put in it vanished – it contained an angled mirror that reflected the emptiness back at you, and everything was hidden behind that. I think he enjoyed this stunt more than the holiday. He never liked travelling – apart from nearby Bornholm, my father only left Germany twice, once on his honeymoon to Paris, and once to Sweden to view an aluminium smelter he owned. He said, often, that travel bored him, that he had too much to do at home. The truth was, he, like many wealthy people, had become used to being treated royally. He suspected, rightly, that this might not happen abroad, that his magic with money wouldn't work quite so efficiently there. And, of course, nothing reveals ignorance quicker than travelling abroad.

My father liked to work in the forest. When he wasn't

at the factory he chose to be a sort of gentleman forester who kept the rides clear, did scientific coppice work and even fashioned hurdles (after his own design) for the local farmers, hurdles which they extravagantly praised. In the evenings he read digests of scientific journals prepared by his secretary, performed magic tricks or mended rustic clocks at which task he demonstrated infinite patience, holding tiny screws in his big hands, each big finger almost bursting its skin it seemed. Despite all these pastimes my father had a surfeit of energy that only building houses could exhaust. The great house at the lakeside, which de Groote later praised, was just one of several homes he built, and the first he constructed without nails. There was some theory about nails undermining German craftsmanship, the skill of making joints and pegged beams. He claimed it was pure coincidence that a similar distrust existed in medieval times when Lucifer was depicted as the maker of the nails that crucified Christ. My father loved all tools, especially tin-snips, scrapers, billhooks, carving knives, sickles, scythes, spokeshaves and planes. He had a Stanley combination plane sent from America with over a hundred and fifty different blades.

He also liked English split-cane fishing rods. In his bedroom at the lake house he kept a five-metre perch pole and half a dozen Hardy fly rods.

Every May he would climb to the top of the church bell tower in the village and go out onto the roof with his fly-fishing rod. There he would cast across the sky as the swallows and swifts returned from their winter migration. Using a No. 6 silk line and a hook with an imitation mayfly tied to it, he would catch hundreds of the poor birds, sometimes as many as three or four a minute. He would send us around the village distributing the birds as a delicacy to be baked in traditional pies and of course all the housewives thanked us. My father sometimes cooked these birds, exhibiting a cruelty absent in my brother and me – he would gut them while alive to show us 'how the organs function'.

The swallow pie recipe was:

10 swallows (skinned not plucked, even the wings were skinned)
1 swift (likewise)
a curl of bacon, a sprig of parsley
breadcrumbs and onion
piecrust

Salt the skinned swallows and swifts – the secret is in the salting. Salt thoroughly and well or the flavour will be indistinct. Seal the flavour in with light frying. Do not worry about the innards – they cook away to nothing. Mix with the other ingredients. Half cook in an open pot and then top with pie crust. Cook slowly for an hour in the oven. Top the pie with the macabre spectacle of a pair of roasted wings.

It was from my father that I learnt how to work. I helped him clear the thick ivy from the top of one of the high brick walls he had built years before around the kitchen garden. With a bank-hook in one gloved hand, and using the other to rip the roots free, he tore away the entire blanket of ivy in minutes. There was something utter in his dominance of the environment, the vegetation didn't have a chance. Watching him, just once, taught me the essence of work. A lesson I then forgot for fifteen years.

When people were ill in the village they laid straw under their windows so that cartwheels wouldn't clatter so much. Sometimes my father got splitting headaches and all the straw of the village would be used to make the world quiet for him.

He told the same stories often and repeated the same information again and again. In a clock, he regularly as clockwork told us, a steel pinion always wears faster than the brass cog it turns. Small pieces of steel get embedded in the brass and make a saw of it, which cuts the steel to pieces. My father liked that one but I don't think he ever saw the moral of it.

When he cut himself he would sometimes stand in the scullery and spit the bloodied sputum into the stone splash bowl. Perhaps my father was careless. He had no fear of pain, or so it seemed to me. Once, at the lake house, rather than visit the dentist, he pulled out a troublesome tooth with a pair of rusty pliers from the toolbox in his car.

11

Early on I took to secretly visiting churches and talking to priests. I had a special interest in saints, who, I saw, were magicians who did not have to pretend. It did not seem to me at the time to be a conscious rebellion. It felt entirely natural; that it went against my father was merely an unfortunate, but unavoidable, consequence.

My favourite saint was St Cyprius, who left the mountains of Syria, where he was a shepherd, for the scorching western desert in Egypt. There he lived in a cave wearing clothes made from wood. Each piece of wood was punctured by hundreds of nails, as if he was a fakir, but one who never left his bed of nails. St Cyprius learnt Greek (from St Jerome) when he was eighty years old. He never had children and he despised people who ate cooked food. Despite existing on a diet of starlings and scorpion eggs, he lived until he was ninety. For five years he gave up speaking since he believed everything he said was a lie. For one year he walked around with his tongue nailed to a piece of palm wood, which is how he is often depicted in paintings. Again this was a penance for lying.

My mother once glimpsed the Bible I stole from school but she looked down and said nothing. I read it under the bedcovers with a torch before sleep. I understood with acuity that if religion was true then one would have to be a saint, any kind of saint, otherwise it was not serious. I devised several tests to discover if it was true. In midsummer I left out an old silk shoe for presents (we celebrated Christmas as the ancient festival of the Solstice – even my father didn't outlaw Glühwein and present-giving) – hoping that Jesus would tell St Nicholas to fill the shoe with toys. I even left a piece of cheese in the shoe as a reward for St Nicholas, who, despite this tasty lure, decided to stay well away. I saw at once that this test was flawed and inconclusive. St Nicholas might have other employment in the summer months that kept him away from toys. Another test: God would speak from behind the curtains when the room was empty and dark, but God refrained from speaking. God would save our pet bantam chick from dying: the chick died. After each test my faith was not a bit altered. Instead I merely felt humbled. I saw that God had more important work. When the devil, or, more likely, the image of the devil, appeared in the clouds one day it was a shock, and I could never explain it.

On the day of his confirmation my best friend Paul Wirth, an altar boy, wept from the anticlimax of it all. He had really believed everything would be changed, made holy, catholic and apostolic after receiving the bishop's blessing and repeating the creed. I, despite a strangely immovable faith in the invisible, had known all along that things would be just the same. I knew mystery and the miraculous must lie deeper than mere words.

12

My first attempt at the miraculous was to try to stop time in its tracks. When I was perhaps thirteen years old, I became one of the bell-ringers at the church across the square (I invoked Addison as my inspiration – he praised bell-ringing as a marvellous form of exercise. My father was surprisingly interested and did not oppose me). Over Easter the bells were rung throughout the night. Long before dawn I was woken by my mother. I went downstairs and drank corn broth from a cup. My mother, saying nothing, lit a candle for me from another candle, already guttering on the oak dining table. It was a still night and cold. I put on a heavy coat with big buttons and shielding the flame with my hand I walked along the short lane and across the snow-swept square to the church. I slowed my pace deliberately, watching the dancing flame in the hollow of my hand, feeling the wax drip hot into my palm. I swung open the heavy door of the church and walked through the dark rows of benches to the altar, flickering light cast in shadows and a cold smell to the place, a cold silence on the stone floor and polished wood. The altar was where I came to stand, focusing on the slight smoking flame of the candle. As the wax ran down I pushed it back up, repairing each dam-break around the wick. My faith in something nameless was so strong I believed that time had stopped as long as I could save the wax in this way. I believed that if I could keep the flame alive forever the open feeling in my heart would also last forever. I believed this even as the candle burned low. Even as it guttered, jerking up high and then down, gasping for air it seemed, even then as the flame was dying I had no sense of time passing, even then it was as if I was outside it and everything was happening in the present not moving towards a future or away from the past.

13

I had another vision. I was fifteen, visiting the capital, probably for the first time – this was just before the war of 1914. There was a demonstration of the future of agriculture lead by a parade of steam tractors. That is what I thought they were, in my indifference to the mechanical. In fact they were almost certainly Holt crawler tractors with petrol engines, anyway, these great metal beasts with their clanking chains linking each wheel together towed ploughs and harrows and mechanical seed drills and grass cutters along the wide streets of the Tiergarten, the crowds held back by a few kepi-wearing policemen between the tall trees on either side of the avenue. One of the tractors broke down, its engine wheezing and stricken in the path of those crawling behind it. With lumbering care, which I saw damaged the road surface, the tractors separated and slowly passed their fellow beast that had fallen in the mechanical progress.

The drama of this slow pageant held the crowd. There were thousands of people watching. And after the tractors and their equipment came motor cars, all privately owned, they had been asked to join the end of the parade. The noise and smoke was almost worse than the agricultural machines. I saw that the drivers, most of whom wore leather-padded goggles to protect their eyes, were grinning maniacally to each other, teeth bared or so I imagined, since most had their faces covered with scarves. Their motor pageant, charged with the artificial life of engines, limited and simplified the crowd and reduced them to the role of dull onloooker. A common observation, but, in this case, true. I grew more detached. It was as if I could turn the sound down of the passing vehicles until they were as in a silent film. They became insubstantial, mere shadows, whereas the crowd became a network of lines and shapes joining the people in the most complex of patterns. This, then, was the vision: for that brief moment the relationships between people were more real than outward forms, material things, shells and husks and containers. The mechanical things, which had seemed so real, became as nothing, the smallest boy sitting on a kerb with a paper bag full of seeds was a tessellation of care and attention, involvement, trust, growth and awareness of others, present or not, I saw the lines like an endless string linking everyone, more and more of it, blackening the page of my vision, until the crowd emanated as the only thing alive and real and nothing else counted.

This vision drove me into the hands of those who I took to be the keepers of God's word. I had finished school and quite against my father's wishes I chose to enter the local Benedictine monastery.

My father had been out fishing for swallows that day, the day I told him. He sensed what all fathers fear – that he had been irrelevant in my upbringing. But typically he chose to ignore me and sat like a stone at the dinner table saying nothing.

14

I loved the heaviness of my new robes, the brick-built cloisters, the enforced silence at mealtimes, even the weak beer which I had rarely tasted until then.

But almost immediately, within weeks of unpacking my few things in the cell, I began to feel a new echoing beat to my heart, a sound like the slapping of wet mud with the back of a spade. I could not sleep. Chest pains made it impossible for me to sing vespers. Even the most worldly of the brothers (and many monks are surprisingly worldly) lost his hale indifference to my condition. I was ill, that was obvious. The strange doctor who attended the monastery, a lay brother who lived in the town below with his mute sister, came and examined me. He tapped my chest with a device like a round-ended bone, listened to my pulse at the wrist with a stethoscope and announced that the rigorous hours of monastic life would surely kill me.

I knew the power of prayer and wondered, then, if this was its reverse. Was my father's displeasure enough to kill me?

To celebrate my return he rowed us all in his aluminium boat to the island in the lake. We ate our lunch at the foot of the rock – the great rock that protruded from the island. After our picnic he climbed the peak in bare feet, as he always did. On the very highest part, stripped to his underwear, he looked up as if searching the skies, or daring the wrath of the heavens. He caught my eye and for the first time I understood there was not arrogance, but a kind of brave humility in going against the Gods.

Then he dived, straight down twenty metres, his arrowed arms protection enough it seemed as he surfaced after an age and broke the clear translucent waters, lordly and laughing fit to burst. Though my brother did jump, no one else dared dive.

I recovered, or at least my heart did, almost as soon as I climbed the stairs to my old room with its view at the back over the water meadows. From my tiny window I listened for the faint sound of the stream, ever present, winding its way through overhanging grasses, through the fields and into the river and away to the sea. I planned to either run away to sea or return to the monastery when I was fully better. Instead letter D601 arrived sending me to the Western Front.

15

Destiny is simply what keeps you on a path, a straight path. A wise man, if you can find one, will indicate the right direction of such a path. If you ignore him, if you fail to read your heart correctly, if you fail to scry the signs around you then you will be whipped in the face by destiny. Illness, injury, mental derangement, pain, all become your teacher.

I served in the artillery, away from the real fighting. Two years and not a scratch. Then in 1917 I was given a new job. Spotting enemy gun positions from an observation balloon tethered behind the lines. We were in a wicker car beneath what was called 'a swallow' (an irony not lost on me), a bulbous dainty observation balloon, patched with silk, going up a kilometre and a half into the sky on a cable far above the pattern of trenches and blown earthworks.

It was really rather pleasant, though the enemy, Scotsmen in kilts that snagged and tore on our impenetrable barbed wire (wire so densely laid you could not see light through it) used to explode shells near us from time to time. In the balloon you could see the puff of smoke from guns, the soft sound of a shell exploding, the distant crackle of rifle fire. Up there, with the roads so thin and the trench lines so narrow, and everything so green despite it all, one could almost forget the war, though my companion Lieutenant Hoeningham delighted in pointing out all the church spires our guns had torn and buckled.

We had a mess can of hot coffee, some brandy, and despite the proximity of the gas we smoked continuously, as if our lives depended on it. Lieutenant Hoeningham gave vent to his outrageous opinions far above the battle. He despised all generals and told me long tales of his seduction of village girls when he was but a lad. 'With hair this long,' he showed me in stark contrast to his bald bullet head, though he did have a non-regulation tuft under his lower lip.

Hoeningham appeared to like me, and, one day, his dark brown, almost gypsyish eyes, contrasting with his worried frown, scanned mine and were satisfied. 'I trust my instincts,' he pronounced darkly. He came from a prominent Munich brewing family all of whom he disliked. 'My only real interest I can tell you now is black magic, the arts of Al-Kemi, literally the "black land", the name of old Egypt.' Up there in the balloon basket he had a captive audience.

'Suppose you were to inscribe a pentagram in chicken's blood, on, say, the concentrated feedstuff of a mule. That mule would die – keel over and drop dead – within a matter of months.'

'Months?'

'Weeks, even. Days if it was particularly weak-minded.'

'A weak-minded mule?'

'Exactly. The war is quite simple,' expounded Hoeningham, throwing his arm wide over the empty air outside the basket, 'a devastating build-up of sexual energy demanding release – and this by God, is it!'

I was too stunned to reply.

'For years there has been a creeping denial amongst the bourgeois classes of Germany, France and Great Britain that sexual relations even exist. Instead a prolix version of a neutered reality has been rammed down the gullets of four generations of young and virile men. Marriage takes place among the officer classes at a late age, almost at the end of a man's breeding career. England had an empire to sate this blocked lust for penetration, Germany and Austria did not. Hence this bloody fucking mess!'

'What is the solution?'

'Solution! Solution! You talk like all of them. There is no solution. The orgy must reach its own conclusion. The climax must happen. Then, of course, the rapine will follow.' He grimaced joyfully at the thought of the rapine that would follow.

'There is a man in England called Crowley. I have studied with him in Scotland, at a magical seminary called Boleskine. He himself was a student for twelve years in Egypt, seat of all the mysteries of the earth. Crowley instructed me in the work of Abrabellin the Mage. He taught the first requisite of the true magician.'

'What's that?'

'To be able to predict the future. For example . . .'

BANG! Loud enough to burst an eardrum, fracture a bone, reverse the blood flow, stop the heartbeat. Think of the loudest noise you know, then double it and double it again. You can feel the blood filling both earholes. The rest of what you hear is simply like a variation on the ensuing silence. Swish, rip, a whistle, a tearing shriek of fabric R—R—R—I—I—I—P—P—P. What was happening? The balloon was hit and falling; the envelope swamped on top of us. I fought at the mountain of rubberized silk and uncovered the face of the nascent Black Magician. 'Jump!' he shouted.

I dived over the edge of the basket and nearly dived straight out of my harness. With a sickening sensation the leg loops slid past my knees and almost right off as I plunged head downward. I grabbed a rope in front of me. By chance it was the rip cord which was toggled to the waist harness. The parachute started to open with an irresistible deadly pull but the cords tangled around my neck strangling me in midair. My face felt swelled to twice its size, my eyeballs became too big for their sockets as if ripe for dropping out like plums. I was nauseous and could not breathe and then suddenly I was freed, though my neck was raw and bleeding from the lacerations.

Now I was falling very fast, with fluttering bits of silk and cord all around me. I thought that this was the end. I saw only blue sky and wisps of cloud. Then, oddly enough, images of people I owed letters to crowded across my mind. I thought, 'Is this what people mean when they say your life flashes before you?' I shut my eyes and kept falling, falling far further than would seem possible and with my eyes firmly shut, I . . . CRASH. My shoulder hammered through my body into the ground. My eyes, though, still worked. I opened them. I was still in the air.

I was still falling. In my headlong dive I had been saved from certain death by landing on Lieutenant Hoeningham's parachute, which, now, promptly collapsed. 'Sorry!' I shouted. 'Doesn't matter,' he said, 'though you could have aimed a bit better. It's not as if there's a shortage of space up here.' Either through ignorance or bravado he kept his humour, you have to admit, even on the brink of disaster. His parachute half re-inflated, half billowed out, spilling air, the wind making a flapping roar. I began to slide down and off his canopy and as I tumbled clear I seized hold of something, probably ten or so supporting cords, so that his parachute was now holding two. Actually I think it was now that he made his crack about aiming badly. As the manual said, double the weight didn't mean twice the rate of fall, but it was faster than usual. My last piece of luck was to hit the ground first with the Devil's representative on top. 'WATCH OUT!' I shouted as his grey-trousered backside bore down on me and then I blacked out.

16

I awoke at the clearing station with a broken foot and a badly sprained ankle, each in its pristine plaster, my trousers cut to accommodate. But my worst injury I did not at first notice. Next to the clearing station was a shed full of sawn-off limbs. I was wheeled past it as an orderly tried in vain to shut the flimsy wooden-planked door against the overflowing naked legs and blood-speckled hands. I tried to say something but could not. I was 'shell-muted', officially 'aphasic': my next destination the hospital for the mentally jarred. It was then that the true awfulness of my affliction came home to me. I could smile, but could not laugh. Not a sound came out of my mouth.

Serious maladies induce panic. I slept badly with nightmares. I made a vow that if I ever regained my speech I would never lie again.

I could write with a pen and paper, but I could not say all that I wanted. I discovered that the unafflicted wait for a while, treat you with kindness because you are ill and say everything in a slow, loud voice, assuming an inability to speak also means deafness and stupidity. Though to be fair, when a man is blown up and loses his voice he is often deaf from the blast as well.

'Speechless with horror', though my own experiences

were hardly horrible. One fellow patient was sleeping in a hut which was blown to pieces by a shell. His five companions were killed instantly. He ran, screaming but not making a sound. He was cured in a week by hypnotism, but he stammered for a month after that.

There were dark Gothic arches in the wards. Many of the doctors smoked meerschaum pipes as they performed chest surgery. I learnt to distrust them all. My mother and sisters visited me on five occasions bringing lilies and heavily scented tulips. My father, though, was needed elsewhere. In the government offices of war production they had set aside a telegraph printer and three operators just for him. Though fantastically busy, he did what he thought was the best for me. He found a new hospital by his rule of three. Ask the three best-qualified people you know and then decide immediately. He asked the family doctor, the head of the medical service and a surgeon he'd twice hunted wild boar with in Silesia. And so I was moved to the finest hospital for the new illnesses of war. The building was designed by Gropius and was devilishly hot in the summer. The young efficient doctors suspected an organic cause, that some physical damage had occurred to make me speechless. I was forced to inhale small quantities of chloroform from a muslin cloth. This only served to inflame my lips and nostrils.

I was surrounded by other incurables. Willy, an oldish soldier who I had to dissuade most nights from clambering into my steel bed with me, was an hysterical hiccupper. (When I pointed out my bed was not his, he would meekly accept this and go back to his own muttering 'So sorry, so sorry' in between hiccups.) He could speak, he was the only one of us who could, but he suffered terribly from his hiccups and this disoriented him in general. His hiccupping started with a trench mortar exploding overhead mortally wounding his friend who gave two shrieks and tapped him on the right shoulder as he fell. Willy ripped the shirt apart on his friend's back and saw a lump of shrapnel embedded next to the vertebrae. He attempted to pull it out and burnt himself: the shrapnel was red-hot.

Eating and drinking made his hiccups louder and more spasmodic so he ate off his metal tray in snatches, as if hiding the fact of eating from himself. If he grew excited he'd hiccup two hundred times a minute. He liked to keep the chess set next to his bed and if another patient took it without asking he would hiccup so violently you couldn't understand him. When he was relaxed the hiccup was silent and the doctors said the larynx hardly moved. He was given bromide and chloral treatments regularly but they did little good. He had been hiccupping non-stop since the Second Battle of Ypres, that is, for thirteen months. He even hiccupped in his sleep, though Willy claimed he never did sleep.

If I ever felt self-pity I needed only to observe Willy or another hopeless invalid, an ex-reservist we called 'Six sixty-six man'. He had lost his memory, his ability to speak and even the power of his limbs. He was also regarded as a wonder, the first case recorded of complete amnesia – not just memory and mental skills, but everything – he had no sense of taste or tactile perception – he would touch the red-hot lid of the stove, burn his hand and then examine the blistered flesh with interest and no apparent pain. He could see but had no notion of what he saw, his limbs were heavy and inactive; he soiled himself like a new-born infant. After months and months he had made some progress, learning a completely new personality along the way. He occasionally suffered from toothache. He regained control of his bladder and rectum. But though he learnt how to whisper, his memory loss was so complete he had to relearn language again. In this he chose a form of pidgin rather than correct speech. It was as if he distrusted the old ways of speaking. For him all forms of liquid were coffee. For petrol poured into a car he called out 'table has coffee'. All vehicles were known as tables. He only had two numbers, one and six, except very large numbers were sixty-six and the largest number of all was six sixty-six.

What a heartbreaking laboratory of the human machine! It was here that destiny ripped up my old ideas about how the mind and body worked. Some died and some, condemned as dying by the doctors, made miraculous recoveries. Something more than faith was involved but I did not know what.

After much investigation it was discovered that my vocal cords were paralysed and not my tongue. A course of hypnosis was tried but I was not receptive, nor did I, deep down, want to be.

Finally, they turned me over to Dr M. The doctor had a head like an angry pustule, with a mouth visibly empty of several teeth. The one remaining incisor hung in doubtful position like the last milk tooth of a six-year-old. I fought the temptation to reach up and snatch it out. His hair was thin and side-swept over a balding cranium. He had watchful eyes, a sudden loud laugh and a skin thickened by success and skill at office politics. He always wore a yellow tie and was imbued with a deep pessimism that was almost palpable: optimism, to him, was something humorous or even shameful, like an adult believing in angels.

Dr M was a student of Freud, but heavily influenced in early life by both Fechner and Weber. Fechner's law was his mantra: 'as the strength of a physiological stimulus increases geometrically the psychological stimulus increases arithmetically'. (Not surprisingly Fechner's work was later appropriated by students of torture.) From Weber Dr M imported the idea of the just noticeable difference between two stimuli, which is proportional, not surprisingly, to the magnitude of the original stimulus. From Freud he inherited a framework, but he had developed his own psychoanalytic technique for probing the unconscious. While Freud focused on language, Dr M looked at the whole body. The twitchometer was his own invention, a wooden structure resembling a crucifix, almost as strongly made, with holes and wooden pins to fit it to the victim's body. Strapped in at the waist and chest, the slightest movement resulted in iron bars that ran along the reverse of the wooden superstructure, and to which one was connected, picking up and amplifying any 'twitch' and this was recorded on a revolving drum of paper. The twitches were correlated against numbers that corresponded to zones of the human body. One was strapped in completely naked to the twitchometer and then assaulted for at least an hour. Dr M had something that resembled a slide-rule with two pins sticking out. This he called the 'fakir stick'. He altered the distance between the pins and struck the body repeatedly, favouring the exposed regions of the buttocks, the genitals and the earlobes, places where 'Weber's ratio broke down in a most interesting fashion'. A sadist in the cause of science, Dr M had perfected, in his mind, a casual gesture, something between flapping and prodding, that settled the two pins into flesh to produce pain but no blood. Often this was not successful and my body was soon punctured all over with tiny red dots. I begged regularly for release but the doctor merely smiled, adjusted his stick and batted me harder.

The twitch map of my body was compared with his archive of former victims. My 'type' was identified. The fall was not the cause. My 'stimulus shield' was badly formed, insufficiently 'baked through' to use Freud's term. Dr M believed that life produces a dead layer around the organism, a carapace which shelters the sensitive soul from excessive stimuli. A 'well-baked', as opposed to half-baked, stimulus shield was the result of a healthy childhood, preferably, Dr M hinted, an unhappy one, not the wealthy sheltered one he assumed I had led.

The twitchometer was right about one thing only – my aversion to pain. 'A good pricking never hurt anyone,' said Dr M, meaning, of course, it never hurt him to administer such pain.

A despised fellow patient came to my inadvertent rescue. He was a young engineer, suspected by the staff of faking mental illness. Using a key he had stolen and copied, he broke into Dr M's office and strapped himself into the twitchometer having placed his erect penis between the wooden 'limbs'. A whole drum of paper, highly rare during wartime, was expended in recording his exultant orgasms, the most tremendous of which broke the machine.

I was allowed home for a visit, while Dr M supervised repairs. For the first time I ceased to feel pessimistic about my condition – which was either the effect of being in familiar surroundings again or the result of making a new friend. A little older than I and an ardent socialist, we went on long walks with frequent rests (ostensibly for conversation). I did not have to make the first move, she did. I knew little of the subtler aspects of intimacy but she set me straight in a charming way, tolerating the clumsy clatter of my teeth against hers, my quick, inept intrusions. With typical youthful pride I thought myself rather a fast learner considering all the misinformation I had acquired in the trenches. After a month of these lessons I first whispered and then with a joyful croak I sang. I was cured.

The war ended but Dr M did not disappear. He went on to enjoy considerable success under the patronage of the high-ranking cranks in the party. Later he was disgraced when it was discovered that he circulated amongst his cronies nude photographs of famous women suspended in the twitchometer. His wife divorced him, the university hospital sacked him and I heard, years later, he took, appropriately, employment as a park keeper with a pointed stick for collecting litter.

Lieutenant Hoeningham recovered completely and went on to head the army parachute-research institute after the war. He never went to Egypt as far as I know. But I did.

I'd been indoors for far too long. Time to face the world. I drove east in my little hatchback, to the other side of town. After patrolling the streets, looking for a parking space, I squeezed into the tail shadow of a huge BMW SUV, black, with blacked-out windows; the drug-dealer's car of choice. My car looked like a boiled sweet left on the pavement compared to that angular monstrosity, which suggested some kind of stealth technology clothed in a black condom. A mobile bunker, though I was loathe to admit it. And it probably was a drug-dealer's car – I was in London's fashionable Brick Lane area for a lunchtime party given by my friend Cheryl Arondice, who I mentioned before but did not add was also the girl of my dreams.

Cheryl and I have been friends for a long time and I have attempted to improve this situation several times, but to little avail. On that particular day I bought on the spur of the moment a spray of pink service-station carnations to go with my bottle of high-alcohol-content Australian red. I felt there was something both pleasing and ironic about the flowers.

On the way to parties I sometimes plan what I am going to say. Often I never say it, but the planning seems to put me in the right frame of mind for saying unplanned things.

The planned topic: the other day whilst walking through London marvelling at the number of houses with giant skips outside, each skip fed by a long tube of bottomless buckets chained together, as if the guts of the house were being sucked out to leave space for yet more tiny flats, I came to a stunning conclusion: build underground! If only troglodytism became socially acceptable the housing crisis of Britain could be averted. If people were allowed to burrow into the sides of hills no farmland need be sacrificed (apart from the negligible area of hobbit-hole entrance) and no beautiful fields need be (much) disfigured. I made a mental note to phone my sister who works for the Environment Agency and would know better than I the exact details of whether or not digging your own burrow was allowed. I knew that in Coober Pedy, Australia, a town I would love to visit, everyone lived underground owing to both the excessive heat and the fact that the town was built on an opal field. Just digging the hole for your house could pay for it. And the Coober Pedyites even had swimming pools underground cast in waterproof concrete.

Not that I was sure that I wanted to relinquish living in London to go and dig a hobbit hole in Herefordshire just yet, but I liked the idea of it being at least possible.

Cheryl's own solution to the housing problem was to live in a rent-controlled housing-association terraced house in the most desirable part of the bohemian quarter of London, right around the corner from Gilbert and George's favourite cafe – though I'd gone off that cafe a little after seeing their flying-shit paintings. Cheryl even had a garden, mainly concreted, but large, and shared with other bohemians who lived in the terrace. The back wall was high and impressively shrouded in a loose net of barbed wire and blackberry bushes. Pretty secure, I'd say. Her front door was another story – it had a letterbox big enough to get your hand inside and a frosted-glass window of smashable size. Cheryl didn't care, though; she considered excessive worries about security a sign of excessive worry. But then Cheryl was one of those lucky people who get beautiful minimal-rent dwellings effortlessly offered to them and never suffer break-ins.

Cheryl earned money as an art therapist. She had two part-time jobs which still left her enough time to make towering metal sculptures of women. She herself was tiny and perfectly formed, but her sculptures were huge, rusty and ungainly, likely to tear your skin if you brushed too close.

I walked in with my carnations and saw immediately that Richard aka 'Dick' Bradawl was also in attendance. I had seen him from afar on two previous occasions, not difficult as he was tall, well built with curly blond hair and a sunburned face. He was also immensely wealthy due to his highly sought-after skill, which, I understood from Cheryl, was 'inventing new forms of debt'. A banker.

I patrolled the party, indoors and out. Cheryl had a work in progress on display and already it bore the telltale sign of threads snagged from the clothes of people getting too close. It struck me that the only person I knew who could weld was a petite girl of five foot one.

I spoke at some length to the almost well-known Colombian artist Freddy Boleras (who had been a professional footballer before getting injured – his most famous work was a Jimmy Choo shoe with football studs). Freddy was drunk and just leaving but he invited me to his forthcoming show at the prestigious Coalhole Gallery. The Coalhole is underground and has all its pipework showing – an artbunker with pretensions – I liked the place.

With a certain recklessness brought on by a few too many glasses of high-alcohol wine, I engaged Dick Bradawl in a discussion on troglodytism, hoping (in a very vague way) he might have the money to fund Britain's first troglodyte new town. Instead he took a leather cigar case from the inside pocket of his silk-lined blazer. There were three Romeo y Julietas in the case but he did not offer me one. After sparking up and inhaling he pronounced, 'Wouldn't work.'

'Why not?'

'Just wouldn't. Holes are too damp.'

End of conversation.

By this point I understood via the hubbub around the kitchen table where Dick was lounging that the immense floral display, to which my carnations were integrated not unimaginatively by deft Cheryl, was courtesy of Dick's country estate, farm, cottage, whatever, from which he had just come that very May morning.

I regarded Cheryl with a sort of panic. Had she succumbed to this oaf? Nothing in her demeanour suggested she had, but the very presence of this large awkward twat whose flowers were as unironic as you could get suggested his advances had not been repelled.

I realized then and there that I would have to make a greater effort to secure Cheryl otherwise she would be lost to the likes of Bradawl. For ever. Luckily Bradawl made one huge faux pas when he asked to see the cricket 'just to catch up on the score'. 'I haven't got a telly,' smiled Cheryl brightly. 'I'll get you one,' said Bradawl. 'I don't want one,' said Cheryl.

But this small triumph over philistinism was short-lived. Just as I left the house I saw a shopping trolley being pushed by two boys with a third sitting inside it careering down the pavement. Swerving wildly they hit, accidentally on purpose, my car, scratching the door and knocking the wing mirror so far back it wobbled and then fell off. 'Oi!' I shouted without conviction. This was not merely cowardice: once I was challenged for no reason by an eight-year-old who wielded a piece of two by four he picked out of skip. Even an eight-year-old can do damage with a big bit of wood. One of the childish miscreants looked back briefly and his smug smirk communicated 'I'm not worried by you!' and on they thundered skidding and hitting another car before turning out of the street. As I stood trying to fiddle the snapped wing mirror back into position Richard Bradawl appeared and laser-clicked his car from a distance – the black BMW flashed all its lights simultaneously like a spaceship about to take off. Bradawl patted me on the shoulder and grinned. 'Bloody terrible neighbourhood this, isn't it?'

Then he was inside his outsize Tonka toy gunning the 12-litre engine, and off.

Why hadn't the tiny hooligans damaged his car? Obviously because they feared the repercussions of damaging a drug-dealer's wagon.

Driving home with the wing mirror as my forlorn front-seat passenger I reflected on the sad fact that the drug dealer has become the current urban role model of choice. Dick had the car, I had the door.

When I got home, I felt disturbed for some reason. I couldn't settle. I practised 'neem' as a form of distraction. An awful upwelling rumbled through my gullet. This nausea, which Hertwig never mentions, made me conclude I was doing something deeply wrong. I did a few aluufs and be-atts for good measure, croaking like anything. It felt good, for a brief moment. A bit like that strange sensation of freedom you get when you think you've escaped a well-deserved hangover – then bang. I ran to the bathroom and promptly threw up Cheryl's vegetarian nut bake. Every last bit of it.

With my heart beating too rapidly, I contemplated the flushed loo in a sour-tasting quandary. Did I throw up because of some terrible flaw in Cheryl's nut bake or was it the result of practising the Universal Language? I needed to know for sure. I went and got the photocopy of Dr Ragab's book and looked up some more letters.

On the first page I again saw and ignored the warning against unsupervised learning.

Gwyn – *Squat down on all fours with one's backside in the air, legs and arms straight, then stretch forward like a cat. Expel the sound at the end of the stretch.*

Easy peasy.

Gees (hard G) – *Legs slightly apart, slowly descend by bending at both knees.*

Nothing to it.

Daal – *Make two fists and extend each thumb upwards. Imagine each thumb twice as long as it is.*

Not as simple as it sounds. Think Chinese mandarins.

Lam – *Extend both arms forwards and then twist first to the left and then to the right. Visualize lines of light coming from each arm. Repeat five times a day. Repeating the alphabet of the Universal Language is like a musician practising scales.*

Yeah.

Tain – *Rotate the head and neck forwards duck fashion. Use this motion to repeat the word many times.*

'Tain' was almost addictive. I performed duck-head manoeuvres until my neck ached. Then, after stretching forward like a cat twenty times and exhaling gywn, I lay down on my bed, utterly exhausted. When I awoke ten hours later I had one of the worst cases of the flu I've ever suffered.

Ignore a warning – learn the hard way.

I reflected, in my fluey thick-headed state, that I had never altered my behaviour one jot because of something I read in a book. Maybe it was because I was a member of the TV generation. Once when I was about thirteen I watched a rerun of the 1950s movie *Bad Day at Black Rock* with Spencer Tracey, in which he plays a one-armed war hero. In one celebrated outburst of violence he knees a bad guy in the stomach and then karate-chops him across the back of the neck. The very next day at school I did exactly that to a mild-mannered and unthreatening boy called Chris Pole. For no reason. Just because I'd seen it on TV. It was completely out of character too. I was a swot not a hard nut. But for that moment the spirit of Spencer Tracey had possessed me. Or the spirit of TV. Anyway, no book had ever had the same effect. In a way I thought of books as neutered. Though I liked them. Though I made a living from them.

Neutered. Until now, that is.

I picked up *Nemesis* by Agatha Christie, but the (neutered) comfort I thought I would derive from reading about Miss Marple turned into irritation. Maybe Poirot would have been more soothing.

In between lying in bed and making and sipping hot lemon and aspirin drinks I fell to further pondering. My life was wrong, attenuated, thin, one-dimensional. There was no relief, in every sense of the word. In the past I had laughed more, appreciated everything more. But as I got older I became more focused, better at getting things done but more miserable. I could see no solution: when you dwell in the bunker a bit of the bunker dwells in you.

Mine isn't a world in which Coelho/Hertwig-type events are likely to occur. I am open to suggestion but rooted in scepticism.

My mysteries are in the past (Why did they build Stonehenge?) or the future (Will global warming flood London?). The evidence of vomit. The evidence of flu.

Cheryl rang and offered to come round but I refused. There are few things less erotic than the site of an unshaven man in three-day-old pyjamas surrounded by snot-filled tissues. We agreed to go for a walk along the South Downs when I was better. She said she had a funny thing to tell me about Dick Bradawl. I asked what but she said it would have to wait. It was worth it, she said.

What was the point of telling me that? I tried to put all thought of the moron Bradawl out of my still feverish mind.

What else was I going to do? I picked up Hertwig's memoir.

17

A year after the war I took lodgings in the nearby university town. My father was not encouraging and gave me little money. I'd chosen to study literature and oriental languages rather than the law, which was his preference. I was staying in Scholars' Lane, an overhanging street of narrow rooms with wooden walls imprinted, somehow, with the always dull version of enlightenment promised by academia, the candlelit dingy effort of true scholarship.

During the day I had a rigorous ascetic routine. Rising early, I would polish my notebooks and rewrite them in a fair hand. In the afternoons I sat in the university library, a high-ceilinged room with stained glass and large paired oil lamps at every desk. If you asked, the librarian would light the lamps even during the day. Smoking, too, was allowed, as was snuff and chewing tobacco. It gave the library a well-worn cosiness. I pursued a new path in my reading, relishing best the books that confounded all previously accepted facts, theories, premises and arguments. I sought to challenge my own thinking. Philosophy was my first interest but slowly I began to gravitate towards the mystics and alchemists, the astrologers and soothsayers, the men who held the puzzle of the world in their hands and said it could be solved. It was good to read Kant after that, just for a breath of fresh air. Then back to the Greeks, my old standby, but these new interests were pulling me away.

One cannot study the Greeks honestly without realizing the value of Averroes, Maimonides, the Blessed Ramon Lull, Abelard of Bath and Hector of Rome, the Jews and Gentiles who read Arab translations of the Greeks and so acquired something not in the unadorned language. This whiff of something was what I came to love, it was what I sought, and missed in the later scholarly translations taken directly from the Greek and turned into rigorous German. It was the smell of the East, which I imagined as a real smell, a compote of papyrus, old leather, jasmine, the scent of newly peeled palm leaves, charcoal fires under a night-bright starry sky, guttural voices, the tinkling of camel bells signalling the caravan's arrival, mysterious palaces and monuments; the great remnants and treasures of ages (besides which all the gold and silver trinkets of the Dark Ages look like the night work of a burglar). In short I was drawn to every idea, every story, every myth that sought to depict the land east of the Bosphorus. (Later I would find that many of these were true, but in a way I did not suspect.) I had found the Orient within the old books of the library. In a world where men used TNT and mustard gas to gain advantage, or sold their labour to earn barely enough to stay alive, in such a world the East beckoned with glorious bejewelled majesty.

18

There were few aeroplane services in those days so I travelled by train and ship. The war had eaten into buildings and left its mark everywhere. People were determined to dishonour the old inequalities. In southern Germany I saw rich men mobbed and insulted on train platforms as I sped by. Through the Alps and into Italy I subsisted on hard cheese and bread in floury loaves bought at stations. I filled my tin cup with water wherever I could. I was never sick. Passengers became great friends and then disappeared forever, sometimes leaving behind a piece of their luggage. I had a destination: Cairo. I had considered Constantinople and Damascus, Jerusalem and Baghdad, but each time I chose one of the others I found myself then calculating how I would then go on to Cairo.

Cairo not Baghdad was, for me, the place of a thousand and one nights, and it is true Scheherazade's tale was first collected here. Cairo was all at once ancient Egypt, Greece, Rome, Islam, both Ottoman and Mamluk, the present military occupation by the officious British; a home to Arabs, Nubians, Armenian cotton traders, Syrain millionaires and Albanian concrete magnates. It was the junction of the Nile, the end of the desert, the last outpost, or first, of Africa, ruled by Turks, Greeks, and Circassian slaves. It was there I would seek the Wisdom of the East.

19

In the 1920s it was also a divided city. There were foreigners everywhere in the fashionable centre. Greek café-owners, Italian waiters, English pharmacists, Armenian merchants and Jewish opticians. In this quarter buildings were new, clean and as impressive as, more impressive than, anything in Europe. Boulevards devised by Haussmann were wider than those in Paris. Cars were plentiful, as were the rich. Everyone dressed well, ostentatiously well. I saw no wisdom here.

Then there were the Arab quarters, the old city around Al-Azhar and under the Citadel of Saladin. The streets were narrow and dirty, sackcloth hung over the alleys against the slim chance of rain, women called from up above behind their mashrabiya screens and let down baskets for whey cheese and broad beans.

For a few days I tried to endure, but the great city overwhelmed me. The first thing I bought was a knife, a nasty little knife for stabbing people, a stiletto – the handle was a narrow crocodile in ebony with two little paws at the end, perfunctory paws to finish the handle off. It was not well made but the blade gleamed and was oiled and slid in and out of the ebony sheath with a slick precise feel – I could peel tomatoes or stab a fat buffoon with it, it was a knife full of possibilities and yet before arriving I would never have dreamed of buying such a thing.

The fact was: I was scared. Partly the smell of the place scared me and partly it was the looks I was given by haggard men in torn garments. I felt at such times for my inner tube of money rolled up under my arm. The smell, I instantly knew, was the stink of Africa perfumed by the desert and polluted by the streets and I needed my little knife against it.

To go all that way only to hate the place – what a foolish mistake. I was at a loose end and didn't know what to do. I took lodgings in the native quarter of Gebilaya, paying my money to an old Christian Arab with a cross tattooed on the underside of his fat wrist. My room had the largest bed I had ever seen, but it sagged in the middle and was as hard as a sack of stones. I slept badly and dreamed of home.

Looking out of my window there was an alleyway where skinny cats with big papery ears ran after tiny malnourished mice. I several times saw a weasel, quick as anything, run along the tops of parked donkey carts. Rubbish was dumped there but it soon disappeared, after the cats had darted and lingered all over it: palm leaves, squashed sweet-smelling oranges, a collapsed, home-made looking chair. At night something came out and picked everything clean. I didn't yet know that this was one of the innermost secrets of the East.

My days passed in moribund inadequacy. I made no friends. I was shouted at. Once or twice I made threatening gestures back. I decided to learn Arabic but bizarrely could find no shop selling exercise books. I wanted to be upright and respected. I wanted to crawl through the gutter searching for lost pearls. I learnt the script in six hours (I had always been good at alphabets). I was half convinced I had come there not for wisdom but to stumble towards an early grave. I paid a visit to the foreigners' free hospital where the worst cases lay in poverty and were robbed by the turban-clad orderlies. Was I doomed to end up in such a place?

My search for wisdom, as I called it, took me to a quarter in the old city, a filthy place full of flies and possibilities. I shared the company of unshaven men drinking endless cups of transparent tea. For a while a dwarf befriended me and made everyone laugh, even those I sensed were making hostile remarks when we first entered a coffee shop. His devotion to my quest was perfunctory: the first man of wisdom he took me to tugged at my hair in surprise and then berated my poor little friend – apparently the man only dealt with curing cases of baldness.

I found chiromancers, masseurs, herb-doctors and hypnotists. An Egyptian examined my eyes with a handheld mirror and said I would see the future if I treated myself first with a decoction of opium smeared on the lower gums. This was not what I was looking for, this was just quackery. But it struck me for the first time, when I left him, how ill equipped I was to judge the wise man from the impostor.

And then I met Dr Ragab.

20

Of course it was by coincidence. Dr Ragab often alluded to something he called the 'science of coincidence' of which natural science as the West knows it is but a pale reflection. In the science of coincidence certain spots on the planet are host to more coincidences than others. Certain street corners, even.

I was walking down Qasr Al-Aini street in Garden City, a newer neighbourhood full of embassies and grand villas for the rich. I had discovered a billiards hall there frequented by dissolute Egyptians and resident foreigners and once in a while went there to play at someone else's expense.

On the way I called in at Shaheen's photographic shop to collect some prints. Old Shaheen tugged at his grey moustache and giggled and explained my film was not ruined but had been doubly exposed. Had that been my intention? (I should explain that Shaheen had a cheap service where he wound short lengths of 120 film from a big reel he kept in his darkroom. This is how the mix-up might have occurred.) He showed me my sixteen black-and-white pictures taken with my Lumirex camera. They were of all the conventional sites – the pyramids, the sphinx, the Egyptian museum, the Citadel – yet in front of each, or next to the photograph of myself (if I had asked another tourist to take it), stood the ghostly image of Bes, the cheeky Egyptian ancestor of Priapus, a dwarf god with an erect penis extending like a broom handle.

It was an accident, but Shaheen took the blame, though he obviously had no idea how it had happened. Clutching a free film in compensation I went into the billiards hall with its lit green-baize tables and men drinking at the bar.

A dissolute overweight youth sat there and greeted me with a wave of his beer glass. Fakhry, the English-educated son of a wealthy pasha, who I had given 'advanced' German lessons to in return for a free drink and a game of billiards. Fakhry was intelligent and read Nietzsche when he didn't have a hangover. He was also an enthusiastic reader of Stewart Chamberlain, but he was not a typical supporter of the fascist nationalist 'Green Shirts'. Years later he would recruit poor Jews who spoke only Arabic and parade them in front of Goering, on one of his many visits to Egypt, as 'friends of fascism'. A Middle Eastern joke.

I showed Fakhry the pictures. He roared with laughter and told me that this statue was a copy by the well-known (except to me) Egyptian artist, Paul Curiel. He pointed out some vague confirming details. Then he added, 'This statue was designed for Dr Ragab's garden.' Even then, knowing nothing more about the man than his name, I knew it would be at least interesting to meet him.

Fakhry said, 'Dr Ragab is reasonably well known. He speaks German. He invented a machine for . . . well, anyway, something.' Then he gave a grin. 'He entertains well, his parties are . . . are luscious festivals of the female form, a haven of white-breasted women.'

'Have you ever been?'

'No. But rumours abound. Rumours abound.'

I wrote to Curiel, making light of my spoiled film. He replied warmly that he had indeed taken and lost the photographs. How the film ended up back at Shaheen's he had no idea. The statue was for an Egyptian-themed garden the Doctor planned. He praised Ragab in the highest terms, which I took to be mere flattery.

21

In a copy of the *Egyptian Gazette* I saw a photograph of Dr Ragab announcing a lecture he had given on the subject of proto-hieroglyphics found in the Egyptian desert. I had it with me when I was again at the billiards hall with Fakhry.

'He looks very ordinary,' I said. The photograph was of a moustached man with round glasses, and undistinguished chin, perhaps a little plump. Fakhry snorted.

'Don't let that fool you. He's a master of disguise. Like Haroun el-Rashid he gets everywhere. He can transform his appearance into anyone he cares to – a *zebaleen* rubbish collector or a pasha, he can pass himself off as both.'

'What's he a doctor of?'

Fakhry took a sip of cold beer. 'Dr Ragab, Dr Ragab is a doctor of . . . I don't know . . . I suppose he's a doctor of everything.'

I think it gave him pleasure to see a foreigner at last impressed by something Egyptian other than King Tut and the Great Pyramid. (Much later, when I asked Dr Ragab about Fakhry Bey, he laughed. 'He does love stories so I made sure he heard a few.')

Once I knew Ragab's name it seemed unsurprising that almost everyone had heard of him. Cairo is like that.

People hoard information and only let it out when they know you are ready for it. They are generous with time and miserly with information, the very reverse of the busy European dispensing advice to everyone.

Ragab's famous machine was a device for accurately excavating the soft limestone found around El Minya – previously worked by hand. He had built his house of the stuff, a palace I learned, on one of the islands reclaimed in the Nile after the British built their dam. As well as inventing, he had medical skills and was sought after as a consultant in fertility treatment; he also dabbled in psychiatry, an amateur head-doctor with an uncanny instinct for the heart, he cured those ailments the rich are especially prone to. The 'Doctor of Everything' was rumoured to have made a fortune curing King Ismail's young son Abbas of kleptomania – the boy had been such an embarrassment, even pickpocketing Lord Cromer's pocket watch while the British minister spoke of Philae in his execrable French. Dr Ragab had banished mysterious lumps, a pustular rash that had no known cause but disfigured the face of a well-known Greek Egyptian heiress. A man who had all his life been unable to climb stairs for fear of heights Dr Ragab cured in an afternoon. Or so I was told. Mainly the stories were of rich men's children who had gone astray, for which he was always paid in gold – he insisted. Gold was Dr Ragab's preferred currency, dollars and pounds sterling were for bankers and coffee merchants. I imagined him, with some difficulty it must be said, for I still retained the newspaper image of the dapper little man, gloating over his money, his ingots, his doubloons, his sovereigns and his czarist stamped gold blocks, exchanging his skill for ill-gotten gains.

Fakhry Bey told of how, on one occasion, Dr Ragab had used his musical skills to repair a factory machine.

'There was a steam engine operating at a cotton mill, one of the old kind with a single huge cylinder. It became jammed and no one could fix it, none of the French engineers and none of our rather more inventive Egyptian mechanics. It seemed that a new engine was required – a huge expense even for a profitable mill. Then the owner asked Dr Ragab to examine the problem. It was quite remarkable. He walked around the stuck cylinder several times and then asked for it to be surrounded by ten or twelve workers with a talent for music. He specified that they also should each be holding a large hammer. He held one himself. Then he began to beat a regular tattoo on the metal casing, slow at first, with each worker keeping time. He kept each beat for a half-minute before raising the tempo a fraction. At a certain rhythm there was a low hum in the air. Dirt in crevices on the cylinder worked loose. Dr Ragab kept this beat for minute after minute. The humming grew louder and louder and then with a screech of metal against metal the piston broke free. The men, naturally, thought it was magic. Dr Ragab, I understand, explained it was pure science. Something called resonant frequency – soldiers marching across a bridge cause it to tumble down, opera singer explodes wine glass – that sort of thing. It's all connected to him knowing the *lugha 'alimaya*. My father told me.'

'What is *lugha 'alimaya*?'

'Language of everyone.'

'A Universal Language?'

Fakhry shrugged. I had reached the furthest extent of his knowledge.

Like all those who have spent long hours in libraries I knew, superficially, about Universal Languages. They were artificial tongues made up to refine communication. In the seventeenth century many philosophers, including Leibniz, had been tempted to construct them. They hoped to reduce the ambiguity of everyday discourse and make it as accurate and truthful as mathematics. One inventor, Wilkins, claimed lying was made impossible by his language. These were *a priori* languages, completely unrelated to existing ones.

The later languages, such as Esperanto and Idiom Neutral, were *a posteriori*, stripped and renovated Indo-European tongues aimed at promoting unity and world peace.

Later, when I asked Dr Ragab what interest he had in the old European Universal Languages, he told me: 'Almost none. Your assumption is that the East trails the West in this matter. In fact the European languages are just another failed attempt at something already settled in the East long ago. You seek. We, however, have already found.'

22

Quite unexpectedly I was invited to one of Dr Ragab's parties. I had written to him about the photographs and heard nothing for months until the large white invitation arrived.

It was to be held at his palace, on the Nile island of Geziret Dahab. The island was a patchwork of carefully tended fields with a Christian village at one end and a Muslim town at the other. A cross at the north and a minaret at the south. Dr Ragab lived in the middle, close to the edge of the river, his palace surrounded by high hedges and extensive gardens. I took a night ferry there rowed by a Nubian with wrists as thick as bundled papyrus. There was a pathway lit by flaming torches which led to the imposing mansion with its round turrets and extensive Art Deco balconies. Two fat white pillars supported a grand portico, in front of which stood a stern doorman with a torch resting on his baggily trousered thigh. Servants clad in tails and red tarbooshes took my shabby overcoat and opening double doors ushered me into the ballroom.

I hurried past waiters tending a huge, slowly melting swan carved from ice surrounded by ice roses and ice cygnets all sitting on a shimmering bed of sevruga caviar. Above me shone ten massive chandeliers, electric-lit, hung from a high-domed ceiling covered with paintings depicting the entry of Saladin into Jerusalem. Beyond there must have been over a hundred people in expensive gowns and evening wear, not including a fifty-piece orchestra tuning up on a banked stand of seats.

Of Dr Ragab there was no sign.

I wandered through the crowd feeling expansive with a newly acquired glass of champagne. I prided myself on being able to spot people I had heard others speak of but had never met myself. The photograph I had studied suggested that Dr Ragab, I was sure, was this short man standing next to me, skinny, round-backed, a chain-smoker of cigarettes with a wizened grinning monkey-like expression. But looking hard I changed my mind. Perhaps it was that other man, pointed out to me by the shiny-nosed wife of the Norwegian consul. 'That's Dr Ragab,' she said, 'at least I think it is.' He was tall, distinguished in a way certain Egyptian men are, rather commanding and imperious of eye, a straight nose and high receding hairline. His impeccable black suit with tails, white waistcoat and tie looked very good on him, excellent in fact. Unlike his neighbour, the grinning man, whose clothes not only failed to mask but even exacerbated the imperfections of his frame. Yet this marvellous specimen was not Ragab either, I was sure. An Italian general, a man yearning to invade a continent by the look of him, nudged past me for another drink. He wore a white tropical uniform, a splendid get-up I have to say. My own evening dress was borrowed and green with age. I got the distinct impression that the uniform preceded the general and was partly to blame for his bumptiousness. Without the medals and the star-studded epaulettes, several small nations might well still be free. (Stripped to his underpants, his ambitions might have shrivelled to commanding the local football team.) Then I looked again – the eyes were familiar – surely this was Dr R in one of his famous disguises? The general noticed me and glared. No, that couldn't be him.

No one else seemed at all perturbed by the lack of a host. 'It's often like this,' said the Norwegian consul's wife, 'I understand he comes and goes as he pleases. And every party is different.'

A cheery American joined in. 'Yeah, I heard that one time people all had to sit round little tables on the floor – no chairs at all. And sometimes it's fancy dress – but serious fancy dress, people get prizes for looking exactly, and I mean exactly, like a movie star, or a person from history or something!'

A man with a strange-shaped head was openly derisive of this comment. He caught my eye and introduced himself. 'Emil Kasparius.' He gave me his card – he was the agent for a German wire agency. 'But journalism is nothing. My real interests are more diverse.' Kasparius deftly swopped his glass for a full one, the fullest on the tray I couldn't help noticing, and told me he had 'made significant investigations into what could be called pre-sand Egypt. Though no archaeologist believes in a time before the sands.'

'Really, that is interesting.' I meant it too.

'Yes, there is very much that the archaeological community chooses to ignore. The greatest minds are already working on a connection between our inner destiny as individuals and the records left by the ancients. I know that Dr Ragab knows much about this. I consider him a genius, by the way.'

He fixed me with his green eyes, one a fraction larger and rounder than the other, and took a large sip of champagne.

When the dancing started it was formal and dignified, the Europeans taking the lead, women writing in names on gilt printed cards using jewelled propelling pencils. I had little interest in the waltz and its modern variants. The whole atmosphere of the party was starchy and dull, laboured and yet expectant. There was something wrong about it, I knew that, but I could not say why or how it was wrong.

A line of fairy lights illuminated a door in the corner of the ballroom. This led to the delicious cool of an outside terrace. Here the eccentric and unattached were assembled. One man, a thickset Australian, was holding forth on how he had finally tracked 'that Ragab' down and wasn't leaving until he had the 'low down' on oil south of Kharga oasis. 'He knows all right. If he says go for it – I've got a hundred thousand dollars ready to drill tomorrow!'

As if recognizing my recent arrival an elderly man, well groomed, almost certainly English, said, 'This man has an uncanny knack of knowing the one thing about your field that no one else knows; I have here a list of thirty-one things I need to ask him.'

'What kind of things?'

'Oh, technical stuff mainly.' He turned away, perhaps nervous I would steal a trade secret.

A lugubrious-looking Romanian told everyone Dr Ragab had cured a man of leprosy. 'But it is on trust, you understand, purely on trust, I did not see such a thing myself.'

The terrace was only a short distance from the river, but considerably elevated. There was a scent of jasmine and rose, warm night air, as comforting as the softest shawl. Cairo was visible as a star city far away across the dark fields. Dhows went by with the sail lit by a hissing kerosene lamp. Drumming and clapping fluctuated in waves across the waters from a riverside encampment of mud-brick dwellings. There was a green lamp in the minaret at the island's end and a bright slice of a new moon above it, the circle completed by the spectral remains of the old one. Stars, I always looked upwards at the stars in Cairo. Even now, with the electric lighting more widespread, you see a carpet of stars twinkling in their warm black velvet. Then I saw hundreds, including the staggering cloudlike luminescence of the Milky Way.

It was on the terrace that I met Hagar. She was twelve years old, with blonde curly hair and a set scowl. 'Don't touch my head,' she squawked as I patted the curls caught in starlight, I could not resist it in my champagne-enlightened state. She was sitting on the pillared wall of the terrace staring out at the wide Nile and ignoring everyone and everything. I backed away and trod on something that yelped. 'Oh, do be careful of Hamish.' Hamish was a silver-haired cairn terrier crouched at her feet. 'Sorry, Hamish,' I said. Hagar's parents were the fabulously glamorous Jewish Egyptian film stars Moira and David

Helmedy (according to Hagar, 'irredeemable show-offs') who drove everywhere in a fleet of identical ivory-white Bentleys – the other cars filled with retainers and hangers on, nannies and hairdressers. They took Hagar everywhere they went and she resented it. In a year she would be going to school in England. 'I'm glad,' she said, and started ruffling Hamish's ears.

Though the girl gave no outward show of liking me, I grew sentimental. I had it in me then, and only lost it in later years, the capacity to fall in love instantly. And of course I thought her luminosity of soul was simply a sign of youth, of youthful energy and vitality. Only later did I learn that 'youth' has no meaning beyond chronological age, and the qualities we ascribe to youth are present throughout life. What we call the spark of youth is really luminosity of soul, that is born in some but diminishes and dies in others, less lucky or more careless.

She climbed down from the balustrade awkwardly. I noticed the plaster cast on her left leg. 'They're straightening it,' she said, 'they want it perfect. I broke it skiing and they said it didn't set right.' Her face, which was sharply defined but not beautiful, except in a twinkling boyish way, seemed to plead, in a way, for me to make no comment.

On toes, head above the crowd in the smoky ballroom, I looked vaguely for Kasparius but spotted instead the Norwegian consul's wife, who, viewed through the lens of champagne consumed, appeared exceedingly attractive. 'I have this neck pain,' she confided, 'I wonder if Dr Ragab might be able to do something about it.'

The stuffy, formal nature of the party I observed

earlier was still there. Not greatly, but enough to make everything feel a little forced. Circles of loudly talking men had formed, designed to repel those of a lower or different class. Women were seated, expectant on high uncomfortable-looking Louis Quinze chairs. Two servants circulated carrying a small sedan chair laden with a silver platter of different cigarettes. They set it down on its legs and people chose from Latakia, Sobranie, Petersburgers, Player's. The band, all in wing collars, flipped their music without a trace of emotion. Only the man on the kettle drums looked to be enjoying himself.

With my back turned and facing a waiter holding yet another filigreed silver tray of Veuve Clicquot, I might easily have missed Dr Ragab – and I'm sure many did – at first. From a side door on the left a man in a rough smock and a white turban, a typical *fellah*, a farmer from the delta, appeared astride a small donkey. He had a sunburned face, red cheeks and a brush moustache and appeared to take no notice of the crowd. He rode the donkey through the parting wave of people as if they weren't there. Those who saw him stopped dancing and stared.

Halfway across the dance floor the donkey stopped, braced its skinny straight legs and let out a rambunctious fart. Then it plodded on, carrying an unperturbed Dr Ragab away through a side door.

Observe your reaction to such experiences, Dr Ragab said long after the event. *Fansh* – the feeling of a long-held expectation overturned, a buried belief subverted. Whenever you experience it, repeat *fansh*, learn the letter that way.

The Englishman left in a hurry, holding his long list of unanswered questions. And the oilman who wanted a yes or no was saying, 'Now are you sure, hundred per cent sure that was him?' The Norwegian consul's wife looked distracted and rubbed her pretty neck.

But the rest of the party heaved a kind of collective sigh of relief, kicked off its shoes, loosened cuffs and ties, talked more easily and less carefully. A reversing of polarity had occurred. Instead of waiting to extract energy from Ragab they gave freely of it to each other, the social armour that stifled real interaction for the moment unlocked. The orchestra struck up a new medley of raffish popular tunes and the fez-wearing servants fanned through the crowd with yet more trays of drink. And Dr Ragab made no more appearances for the rest of the evening.

Some new and interesting facts: from a definitive history of aluminium I discovered that Hertwig's father, aged thirty and keen to promote the metal, had the last of his good teeth pulled and a pair of aluminium dentures fitted. They were quite the rage, for a while, especially popular among the wealthy Chinese in Shanghai. By World War II people realized they were too soft, ugly and probably poisonous so only poor people wore them. In Changi Gaol the Japanese issued aluminium false teeth to any prisoners who needed them.

I mulled over the image of aluminium false teeth (all grey presumably) and the way they'd get scratched by knives and forks. The changing value of things is fascinating – once salmon and sturgeon eggs were considered inferior eating to pike – not now. Etc. But I was surprised Hertwig never mentioned this key fact about his father's appearance in his memoir. In company photos Hertwig's father had a beard – perhaps that hid them. Incidentally, Freud had a prosthetic jaw (a cigar-smoking-induced cancer destroyed the original) that cost him $5,000 in 1930. In modern money that's like $500,000, an incredible sum that reflects well on the profitability of psychoanalysis. I suppose it was hidden by his beard too.

2) Bradawl has a secret. A few days ago I went with Cheryl in my Peugeot (still minus a wing mirror – they're incredibly expensive) to the South Downs to walk, with sunny irony and humour (as distinct from the serious commitment of the attempt with Jason), a section of the pillbox way.

I hoped, at the very back of my mind (at the very, very back, since Cheryl and I have been friends for such a long time that such thoughts aren't allowed prominence), that the erotic nature of pillboxes might lead to something. This was a long shot even for me. Pillboxes are erotic only in the sense that a public toilet is erotic. No one normal is going to be turned on by the sight of a dark little cavern made of concrete. And it was silly to imagine the ontological thrill of pillboxes would be transformed into something intimate. Stupid. Cheryl is tiny, agile, artistic and loquacious. She likes to listen. She likes to be funny. She likes to sit on her futon cutting out pictures from magazines for her art-therapy work with kids. Not surprisingly she preferred the white horse carved into the chalk on the downs to the two pillboxes we encountered, though she did say the walk was 'different' and 'quite fun'.

Then, in the car on the way back, apropos of nothing she told me Richard Bradawl had a pierced penis. I laughed out of sheer demented nervousness.

'How do you know?'

'He told me.'

'Why?'

'I don't know.'

How could she be so naive? Bradawl with his metal willy had one and only one intention vis-à-vis beautiful Cheryl. I was so incensed I said nothing and drove home observing the exact speed limit.

Back to Hertwig.

23

How I actually became a student of Dr Ragab cannot be revealed at this time. Suffice it to say I did, after some delays and several extraordinary coincidences, too extraordinary to ask anyone to believe, I might add.

All this while I was meeting, quite regularly, Emil Kasparius. He told me of his belief that a man could achieve anything if he set his mind to it – telepathy, time travel, extended life.

I wasn't so sure. And even less once I started my lessons. 'Preparatory studies', Dr Ragab called them. He had not even acknowledged that the Universal Language was anything more than a Semitic lingua franca. But already I knew enough not to probe – he would, masterfully, simply deflect my questions, or just refuse to answer, a benign look on his face, until I grew embarrassed and gave up.

I have purposely not described Dr Ragab's appearance except in general terms. Sometimes he appeared as a hawk-nosed and imperious Bedouin, at others, a moustached clerk anxious to be on his way. He constantly swapped costumes. Often he dressed in ancient fashions, which were humorous. He loved uniforms and had a weakness for great rows of medals. He was not superhuman, he had neuroses and mannerisms, but they had no hold on him, he could easily outmanoeuvre them.

What was the secret? *Fordung* – a way of using one weakness against another, and an acceptance that neuroses exist for a reason.

'There are many traditional stories, what you might call fairy stories, that demonstrate, by analogy, the working of *fordung*,' he explained. 'When an imprisoned princess is to be rescued from a castle and the guards are set against each other, bad against bad, that is *fordung*.'

Ragab hated snakes. 'If you caught me unprepared I might easily run from a harmless sand snake, so after practising *fordung* I set in motion a procedure, a trick.' The trick was the trigger of behaviour, the thing you could control that controlled the thing you couldn't control. Dr Ragab conquered his fear of snakes by observing that the only part of the snake he did not fear was the ears. 'I know they don't have ears, but if you look to where you think there should be ears you see two little dents. By searching for those dents I could always take my mind off what the snake was. I was released from irrational fear.'

Ragab told me he had a painful time trying to give up smoking. It was to set an example to a friend who, despite bleeding lungs, wanted to quit but could not. Ragab struggled until he discovered the trigger for him was sweet Turkish coffee. If he didn't drink coffee he didn't need to smoke. Coffee was easy to give up, it had no hold over him. He simply avoided coffee houses and kept none at home. After that it was easy to stop smoking.

Of course he told me all this while puffing on an enormous Upmans no. 6 cigar.

'Why did you start again?'

'I no longer needed to set an example.'

'What happened to the man?'

'He died – but in less pain than he might have otherwise suffered.'

'Was it worth it?'

'We help because that is what we do. We are helping ourselves by helping others. But only if we do it without stickiness.'

'What's stickiness?'

'Wanting to benefit when you should be just doing a thing for its own sake.'

Early on and in time-honoured fashion I asked Dr Ragab: 'I wish to know what I should do to learn the wisdom that you have learned.' I thought he would laugh but he didn't. 'Observe and obey.' Dr Ragab was sitting in the light brown leather armchair in his library. The standard lamp was lit and cast a pool of light over the low table and large brass ashtray. For some reason he was dressed in the uniform of a medieval cuirassier and was sipping wine from a huge silver goblet. 'You wish to learn, in the old way, to emulate. You've heard exciting stories about the Wisdom of the East. The reality is more amazing than you can imagine, though strangely, not half as exciting. If you wish to learn there are dangers and conditions, as with any study. If you wanted to become a car mechanic you would be warned against tinkering while the engine was running, and you would accept that your hands would be dirty most of the time. We have our own conditions and rewards, neither of which you can know so I will tell you when you need to know them.'

'If I start I have to continue?'

'What do you think?'

I nodded.

Dr Ragab smiled and said gently, 'As long as you stay on the path you'll be all right. But if you fall off it's the devil's own job getting back on again.'

I sensed a difference in his attitude towards me. I asked again, 'Can you teach me what I need to learn?'

'Perhaps. In any case, prepare for a great shock. As a student you belong to me. Do you understand?'

'Yes.'

This time there was no warmth in Dr Ragab's expression as he smiled, only a malicious glint in his eye.

24

I was given a few days to move my belongings to Dr Ragab's house. On the evening of my last day of 'freedom' I was walking to the European quarter along the Corniche with Kasparius, who masked his extreme interest in Dr Ragab with general disquisitions on Islamic mysticism, a subject about which, I have to say, he was very well informed. His fluent monologue was interrupted by a shout from a passing horse-drawn cab, which pulled up with a clatter of hooves. It was Dr Ragab, in a great rush it seemed. I introduced Kasparius, who was glowing with eager anticipation. Dr Ragab just nodded and when Kasparius proffered his hand he very reluctantly shook it as if he were shaking something repellent. Then, ignoring the shocked man, he turned to me, patted the seat next to him, and hammered on the back of the driver's bench. I jumped up quickly and we galloped away towards the old city.

We halted in Moski Street and headed into the *souk*. In minutes I was being taken down alleyways I would have feared to go alone, past murderous-looking men in doorways grasping amber beads in one hand, a callus on their forehead from repeated praying. 'Sign of a hypocrite,' Dr Ragab snarled. I sensed a growing urgency in our flight deep into the night bazaar. We passed carpet shops and spice-sellers, brass scoops shining in the mounds of cinnamon, story-tellers and letter-writers, each with a small zinc pail of ink. Fire-eaters twirled and danced, casting light on their sweat-shined faces, a professional dervish spun in a faultless cone of green silk; I tripped repeatedly on ancient stones pushing up like teeth from the alley floor and still we continued until we reached a quiet courtyard overhung by vines.

A chained bear sat morosely in the corner, its owner drinking tea and speaking urgently to another who replied over the top of his newspaper. Two dwarves played *tawla*, a version of backgammon, which involved banging the pieces down with great vigour. Four musicians, with their instruments on their knees, ouds, drums and a flute, sipped at a milky alcohol, one snapping his fingers from time to time to make a point. A beautiful belly dancer swathed in diaphanous silks walked by but did not halt – the musicians looked up but carried on talking. 'The cafe of the hashish addicts, they call this place, do not breathe the air too deeply,' smiled Dr Ragab. A long-faced waiter scraped table and chairs into position and we sat. Ragab signalled for coffee, which arrived in two small glasses.

'Some of our effects can be achieved with drugs,' he explained, 'but there is always a price. Drugs put you in debt to your body and most are unwilling to pay that debt.

'And there is always the chance of addiction. I don't mention this to scare you. I have little interest in the moral question. Here, take this.' He handed me with exaggerated subterfuge a brown pellet of some kind. With pantomime urgency he gestured me to swallow it.

I did, took a sip of coffee and felt nothing.

Then he snapped his fingers and all the colour disappeared from around us. My skin was grey. The trees black. The lamps burned with white fire. Then he snapped his fingers again and the coloured world returned. But for some reason I could not make out the boundaries of the place – where had the walls gone? Why did the cafe seem so crowded all of a sudden? There was no background only foreground. A man appeared at our table and played on his tongue as if it were a musical pipe. The laughter of crowds filled my ears and then smiling, intruding his face into view, Dr Ragab snapped his fingers again. Unambiguous reality of a remembered kind, but untrusted now, returned. He spoke.

'That pill I gave you is made from honey and ground herbs. Utterly inert. The effect you experienced was pure suggestion. Most of what people think of as their "own ideas" are pure suggestion.'

The next day the lessons began.

Ah, the lessons. The actual way that Hertwig learned what he learned. I flicked through the next few pages and saw that Hertwig had been given a very hard time. It made intriguing reading. For example:

The Doctor, dressed in a flowing white kaftan and an impeccable panama hat, shouted, 'No! Idiot!!! No! No! No! I said jump, not limp upwards!'

I leapt as high as I could. It didn't help that the temperature was over thirty degrees and we were in a shadeless field of tomatoes.

'Higher!' shouted the enraged Arab.

I kept telling myself it was no worse than I had experienced as a schoolboy, except I wasn't one any more. I wondered if I ought to take it, but there seemed to be no alternative.

Overnight Dr Ragab had transformed into a tyrant. I was instructed to live in bare room off a courtyard at the back of the house. Here, and in the surrounding fields, I took my 'lessons', though I was not allowed to call them that (as I mentioned he preferred 'preparatory studies'). Early on we studied jumping whilst talking. Dr Ragab believed my vitality was low (a constant theme). He sought to improve it by making me lecture on Plato whilst jumping up and down. I was soon exhausted but he drove me on with evil-seeming pleasure.

'And P-lato's . . . use . . . of . . .'

'No good,' snapped Dr Ragab. I fought to regain my breath. I could not control myself any longer.

'What has jumping to do with the Universal Language?'

I hoped this would annoy him, or unsettle him in some discernible way. But Dr Ragab just paused, filled the giant briar pipe he smoked from time to time, and replied, 'Everything.'

25

It was my failure to jump that allowed the snake to bite. This is how the mishap occurred. A grey cobra worked its way up the drain outlet hole in the wash house. From there it smuggled itself into a wicker basket of fresh laundry and slipped away when the basket was left on an upper landing. The cobra then slid under the door of Dr Ragab's library where I was dusting and turning the books, a monthly task though pointless, I thought, as Egypt has the best book-preserving climate in the world. I stepped down from the ladder just as the cobra struck. I leapt back but was too slow and, of course, not high enough. The bite was intensely painful and I ran, or hobbled, like a schoolboy looking for Dr Ragab. He was downstairs examining a bowl of mangoes. 'What's all this?' he asked. I showed him my leg. 'Lie down and don't move,' he commanded. Then without a word he marched out of the house, commandeered a rowing boat to take him to the shore and made haste to Cairo's leading doctor for the treatment of snake-bites. En route, and as a precaution, he sent a telegram to the stationmaster's assistant at Asyut, a man renowned for his telepathic cures of snake and rabid-dog bites. (When the wizened stationmaster's assistant received such a message he would write a few words from his secret book in a cryptic script known only to himself and peg the piece of paper on a washing line hanging behind the station. On any day there might be a hundred such pieces of paper fluttering in the breeze.) The medical doctor who attended me applied the latest treatment, but my condition worsened. Deep in the south of the country, roused from his sleep by the night train from Cairo, the assistant rubbed his eyes and dutifully wrote out his spell. The time was 12.15 a.m. At 12.18 Dr Ragab told me I had started to improve and by dawn I simply had a bruised leg that ached terribly.

'I didn't actually believe that hocus pocus would work,' said Dr Ragab as I recovered, 'but evidently you did, and that's the important thing.' Then he resumed the attack. 'There are two ways to learn everything – and that was the hard way to learn how to jump.'

'But why didn't *you* cure me?'

'Too busy trying to teach you,' he replied.

26

Kasparius arrived at the island one day unannounced. I had been instructed by Dr Ragab, who was meditating (which, judging by the snores, often included sleeping) in his study, on ABSOLUTELY NO ACCOUNT to desert my post in the glass cupola on top of one of the left towers. It was a horribly hot day even with the windows wedged wide open for the Nile breeze. I was up there with a large brass telescope on a tripod looking for stars in broad daylight. Dr Ragab had read that the newly formed Japanese air force trained its pilots by getting them to observe stars during daylight. I was to follow their example, even though it seemed, given the short-sighted condition of most Japanese, a most unlikely proposition. Ragab would have none of it, so there I was stargazing in broad daylight.

Kasparius arrived and gave his card to the bawab or doorman, who scuttled away to find Ragab's housekeeper, an Armenian woman whose Egyptian husband drove Ragab's Hispano Suiza. Was Ragab married? He was, but for some reason his wife preferred to live in Alexandria.

Kasparius sat himself on the large bench seat outside to wait. No one came. He rang again. I could see the bawab making apologetic gestures. I knew Ragab was there. The bawab knew Ragab was there. Kasparius knew Ragab was there. Evidently Kasparius took it as a sort of test and sat down to wait. And wait. And wait. He was still there at lunchtime and received only an enamel cup of water as refreshment. By evening, he had begun to look worn out. I thought he might stay the night, but he slunk away as dusk fell and I could actually see the first stars – which meant of course I could leave my post. I passed Ragab grinning in the hallway and peering out from behind the curtain. 'He's gone,' I said with exasperation at his childishness.

'Oh good, the silly idiot sat out there all day!'

'What have you got against him?'

Dr Ragab thought for a moment. 'His head is a funny shape.'

I must have made a face.

'All right. I have nothing to give him. And he, though he may imagine differently, has nothing to give me.'

The next day, we were in the water garden making Universal Sounds. Dr Ragab did not explain, but I surmised that these were sounds that called to something deep within us, something beyond mere words. Later I learned that he was training me for pronunciation of the Universal Language.

'Oiiieee,' screeched Dr Ragab. 'Now do that fifty times.'

I did my best.

'That was forty-nine times, not fifty,' said Dr Ragab when I'd finished.

I wondered what I would have done in Hertwig's position. I imagined I would have been a much better student. Then, after a moment's reflection, probably not.

On the beach of the island Dr Ragab drew in the sand a strange symbol, a kind of Pythagorean 'Y', a variant of the quincunx.

'Copy that symbol perfectly one hundred times.'

He sat in his deck chair whilst his manservant Suleiman arranged an umbrella to shade him. Large trading dhows went by slowly and noiselessly. I chiselled eagerly at the wet sand, counting carefully as I went. Dr Ragab surveyed my finished work.

'Why are they all half the size of my one?' he asked.

I was beginning to get the pattern here. It was about, or seemed to be about, maintaining concentration, or, rather, a certain intensity of involvement in the task – almost despite the absurdity of it all.

Dr Ragab said: 'Here's a challenge. Find your way to the centre of the labyrinth, but in the dark.'

With the single light out, Dr Ragab's library stood in complete darkness.

Shutters on the windows let in slivers of sunlight, but these were doused by the inner blinds of polished mahogany slats. Covering these in turn were thick curtains of red velvet. The octagonal library room was as light-tight as a camera obscura. ('Light damages books,' he always said.)

He encouraged me to move through the place at speed and without a care. This is how *noorfaal* is practised. You must walk as if expecting to knock into things. No inhibition in movement at all, since inhibition blocks perception.

Say the word, wet both earlobes with rose water and plunge into the dark.

I was given a blindfold and told to wear it for a week. By the end of the third day I was navigating around the place rather well. Then I was told to prepare dinner. At the end of the repast, which was lamb meatballs, rice and vegetables, he remarked, 'That is quite the worst meal I've ever tasted.'

Nevertheless, over time, I learnt to anticipate objects I couldn't see. An extraordinary skill yet it only seemed so when I thought about it, and thinking about it made it instantly go away.

'This training serves many purposes,' explained the Doctor, 'by no means the least important is the metaphorical value. For example, understanding how the visible world is given greater prominence than the invisible world. This is especially the case in European languages.'

Dr Ragab planted certain suggestions, certain ideas that would not bear fruit for years, even tens of years. Such an idea is revolutionary in the occident, despite an informal awareness of the process: 'he seeded the notion', 'I planted the suggestion', 'to sow doubts' but none of these adequately expresses the care and fertility of Dr Ragab's ideas. I have learnt, over time, that the value of an idea lies mainly in its procreative power, what grows from it, what it becomes. Ideologies, though seemingly powerful, are not quite what I have in mind. Ideology appeals to a certain mood. It promises to alter that mood. It promises certainty, energy and above all the triumph of the human over the mechanical forces of destiny. Such promises have emotional force, but they require a bath of continual emotional stimulation to maintain them. Ragab's ideas were different. They could be compared to windblown seeds that can lie dormant for centuries. I recall reading about such seeds that lay undisturbed for two thousand years in a great pharaoh's tomb. When it was opened the seeds were planted. Some were inert but many germinated. These grew and produced more grain that was eventually milled to produce bread.

The lessons went on. On a memorable occasion he suggested I wear women's clothes for a day and mingle with the daily shoppers at the bazaar. I refused. 'All angels are neuter,' chirped Dr Ragab.

Every day I had to relate a joke or amusing incident to the Doctor. This was most trying. One day when I had a nasty headache from the sun and the approaching *khamsin* wind I forgot to do so. He knocked and entered my little room.

'I'm not leaving until you think of something funny!'

I could think of nothing. I tried so hard but everything was serious. I burst into tears. In an unexpected gesture he consoled me, putting his broad hand gently onto my shoulder.

27

The next time I met Kasparius he had converted to Islam and joined a dervish brotherhood. He was wearing a conical hat and a flowing green robe. 'Can't stop now!' he called. 'Off to my Tarriqa.'

Later that same day, as if he knew about Kasparius's new religion, Dr Ragab spoke about the Mevlevi dervishes who were the original whirlers. 'They whirl, or did, for a precise reason – when Jalaluddin Rumi went there he found those inland Turks too phlegmatic for instruction. Drink was not indicated in Muslim culture so he prescribed whirling as a way of stimulating them to a point when they might be able to learn something without the intrusion of their ingrained cynicism. Now, most people are the opposite – too excitable, especially your friend, what's-his-name. Whirling will just make him even stranger.'

'So why don't you tell him?'

'Why keep a dog and bark yourself?'

I took that to mean I should tell him. I did. Kasparius lectured me hotly for an hour on dervish trains of transmission, on secrecy and how it cloaked charlatans like Dr Ragab.

Unable to match his vituperation I remarked, 'But he never claimed he wasn't a charlatan.'

'Precisely!'

Kasparius glared at me, swallowed and made an obvious effort to inject a compassionate tone into his hectoring voice. 'Spiritually speaking, what you're doing is a complete dead end.'

That shook me. It shouldn't have, but it did.

28

By day, Dr Ragab never accompanied me outside the confines of the island. But at night he now took me on occasional walks through the city. We prowled through the poorer neighbourhoods, where dust was raised to a fine art. One's shoes sank into the finest piles of it, as fine as silk and just as soft, as deep as one's trouser cuffs, between railway lines that crossed the street, against half-fallen walls, and leaning palms, piled up around the wheels of carts, slowly burying them, slowly burying everything.

After one such ramble through the City of the Dead, a place of tombs where the families of the assigned caretakers had made homes, we stopped at a coffee house near the city wall. We sat amidst the square-topped metal tables with sharp-eyed men gesticulating and talking loudly, whilst puffing on their water pipes. The smoke was scented: apricot, apple, orange and mulberry. Dr Ragab pointed out the tiny, big-eared skinny kittens that padded along the alleyway.

A beggar came towards us, a woman of indeterminate old age, dressed colourfully with a black scarf encircling her face, both eyes so heavily ringed with kohl she looked frightening, the lines down both cheeks suggesting a hard life. In one hand she waved a brass censer that gave off incense when she swung it heavily in front of herself. Dr Ragab waved her away but she came forward intoning what I took to be a religious verse.

Grotesque though it was I found myself becoming sexually aroused by this grim-faced woman. I wondered if she was some kind of chiromancer or fortune-teller.

'Does this old woman read palms?' I asked.

Ragab laughed. 'You Westerners are all the same – superstitious!'

I smiled somewhat nervously and the old woman laughed too, though she could not have understood. Then in an inexplicable gesture of intimacy she wafted incense all over us and then briefly grabbed me through my trousers. Ragab smirked, 'Fertility blessing – not unusual amongst the peasant classes.'

I chose to ignore this comment and fumbled for some silver to make the woman leave, unable to meet her eye.

'Sex energy,' said the Doctor loudly, 'is one of the most powerful *undirected* forces in the world. To be useful it has to be directed – which unfortunately undermines its power. With the intellect engaged we sense its superficiality. That is why *meaning*-based obsessions – religious or otherwise – always batter the purely sexual urge into submission. It was puritans not libertines that founded America.'

The woman had left but Dr Ragab carried on.

'Sex, however, is the balancing energy par excellence. You know the oriental Yin and Yang?'

I shook my head.

'It's what the Arabs mean when they use Moon and Sun

as technical terms. I don't want to get unnecessarily complex, but sex, like humour, restores the balance infinitely more efficiently than argument. Of course it can unbalance it too.' He looked at me sternly, 'I think it's time we got you on to "The Merciful Pigeon".'

I must have looked confused.

Dr Ragab smiled benignly. 'It's a rather splendid sex manual – in Arabic of course – it'll be a good translation exercise.'

As well as translation I was set the task of compiling a summary of Arabic erotica. By now my Arabic, with the help of a dictionary and grammar, was up to the task. Dr Ragab joked that just as the bath, not to mention fine carpets, silk and perfume had been introduced in the West through the Crusades (early medieval Christianity condemned bathing), so, too, it was time to introduce the finer pleasures of sex. He had selected 'The Merciful Pigeon' as of particular interest. The pigeon was the male member, aroused as if just leaving the nest. The book condemned tobacco as injurious to an appetite for women and listed a variety of positions including the frog, sheep, inkstand and turban, and the banyan tree – a difficult manoeuvre best performed with a 'pigeon' engorged by repeated submersion in lime juice.

This stuff about sex makes it impossible to forget Bradawl and his obvious intentions. Over the past few days, I have been brooding long and hard (unintentional phrase) over Dick's pierced dick. The whole thing is distressing, absurd and even amusing at the same time. In a stroke it marks him out as inadequate and yet super-equipped. It's all part of the dope-dealer's chic. He knows that tatts are old hat, even university professors get tatts these days. He knows that an eyebrow pierce looks too studentish, a navel pierce too girly and a tongue pierce too obvious. Nope, Dick is the kind of guy who wants the best, who goes the whole hog; the king of body mutilation and nothing less: the major piercing of the knob, right through the bell end, ouch, no prisoners.

He's got a silver bolt through it, said Cheryl, and laughed.

Bernie the bolt. I had to take my hat off, in one nutty gesture Richard Bradawl had bunkerized his penis.

What does he do at airport security?

Will it corrode through being pissed on?

What's it like having sex?

Cheryl said she hadn't asked any of these questions because he'd seemed too keen to answer them. That's a good sign.

I went back to Hertwig, who had finished translating sex manuals and was now doing more impossible lessons.

29

'Read all these books by next week.' Dr Ragab dropped volumes on hypnotism, psychology, anthropology and travel on the table.

I knew enough to not say I had already read some of the books, or parts of them: I had learnt that lesson before. Dr Ragab had fumed, 'You think one reading is enough? Some books do not reveal anything until the sixth or seventh careful perusal! You think a book is only one meal, something you discard as quickly as you can?'

After reading each book I was asked to summarize its contents in a long poem. I found it rather pleasant work. I think the Doctor suspected this. Books were quickly superseded by more testing material.

'Any fool can ask a question,' said Dr Ragab. I was told that from now on I should never ask any questions. He then sent me to the bazaar to find out the price of vegetables. By standing close to customers I sometimes overheard but I was not successful. When I came back Dr Ragab looked surprised. 'Where are the vegetables?' I immediately realized that buying reveals the price by action not asking.

The lessons went on, page after page. Only a few seemed to be to do with learning the actual speaking of the Universal Language.

Most seemed to be variations on testing how far Hertwig could be pushed.

One day Dr Ragab announced that numbers corrupted us. He explained:

'Numbers have been increasing since the beginning of man's love affair with science and its recent offshoot: inventions of a complicated nature. I myself have taken to noting how many more numbers we have to deal with in these busy times. New numbers include so-called imaginary numbers, logarithms, tangents and so on. In fact these new numbers are like a loan from reality and like all usury, of dubious advantage. Michael Faraday discovered electricity with only a child's grasp of mathematics! Let us be rid of numbers! Not all of them, of course. A few are always quite useful – but do we really need more than ten?'

And so I was told to never use a number higher than ten. It was quite wearing.

Dr Ragab arranged for a boxing ring to be set up in the garden. He entered the ring and sparred with a local tough, receiving a number of blows to his body. As he stepped out of the ring I noticed the red marks on his arms where the blows had fallen. 'You are too hesitant. Amir will teach you how to strike first.' The tough smiled, revealing his gold teeth.

He was gentle with me – at first – jabbing lightly at the leather sparring helmet I was allowed to wear. After several days he forgot himself and let his blows fall more heavily. I hid behind my gloves and tried to climb out of the ring. Then I felt a prod in the back. It was Dr Ragab poking me with his walking stick. 'Back at him, young man, back at him.' With flailing arms and a new resignation I even landed a blow that disturbed the immaculately oiled hairstyle Amir favoured.

After two weeks of this the boxing lessons were stopped. I felt bruised all over but at least I had the schoolboy satisfaction of knowing how to land a punch.

What is it I can't help admiring about Hertwig? His wholeheartedness. People (including me) give up too easily these days.

One day, after hanging from a bar set between two trees, and intoning the Universal Alphabet to his grudging satisfaction, Dr Ragab explained:

'The Universal Language has another role. Apart from being a modified version of Arabic, or even set of magical techniques.'

'How do you mean?'

'The attitude required to "speak" the language, the focused nature of being present in the here and now, also allows you to apprehend, or begin to apprehend, the right thing to do at any time, the right thing for you and the right thing for the world. As all mystical systems promise, there is a noumenal reality, of which our world is but a series of shadows, a hidden reality with a different causal engine to our world of appearances. Hence the science of coincidence. We call them coincidences (or miracles if we benefit greatly) and thereafter forget them. We do not notice that our lives are riddled with coincidence, that coincidence keeps us alive, not probability. In all probability no one should survive crossing a road, let alone a great and catastrophic war. Coincidence is a name we give to a cause we do not understand, evidence of a plan we do not comprehend, a pattern of miraculous doings only half perceived.'

He was dressed at the time in the old smock he sometimes wore around the garden. He indicated that I should drop from the bar and walk with him. As we strolled he inspected the condition of the flower beds.

'Is the Universal Language ever written down?' I asked.

'The words can be. The sounds. But not their real meaning, their inner significance. You can give explanations to one person that might be disastrous for another, so in a way it can never be written down.'

He bent down and broke off a dead flower head.

'But once the language had a symbolic form. Then the inner meaning was set down. Long ago. Very long ago – when these symbols were carved into the ancient Pillars of Seth. Josephus writes of it in his account of the Jewish Wars. Two pillars, one of brick, one of marble. On them was engraved the wisdom of the age as a guard against the flood. Later they were lost, though Josephus claims he saw the brick pillar half buried in Jerusalem. That is now gone but I have seen the marble, or stone, pillar in the desert west of Dakhla Oasis.'

'May I see it?'

I expected the usual rebuke.

'I don't see why not.'

And that's how we embarked on the journey to see the Lost Pillar of Seth.

'Mind you,' the doctor added, 'it won't do you a bit of good.'

Still thinking too much about Bradawl. I decided to up my campaign for Cheryl's heart by inviting her to a reading at the Swedish Embassy by my favourite author, Sven Marquist. Obviously this is a dumb thing to be doing from the viewpoint of conventional seduction but I had long favoured the idea that pretending you're someone you aren't is a recipe for disaster with women. At the very least it puts you in the same category as berks like Bradawl.

Anyway I had been looking forward to the event for weeks. Sven would be reading from his new book, *A Short History of Bodybuilding*. In it he cleverly intertwines an account of his own addiction to bodybuilding (despite being sixty-eight) with a history of muscle-cultivation. Sven's books are full of strange imagery, often from the desert and his childhood, involving babies and cactuses, stuff like that. It's hard to pin down but it works in a kind of post-apocalyptic way. His hatred for his father always shines through, de rigueur for an intellectual his age, forgivable in Sven because I like his style but so passé. (Goddam it, our fathers are all we've got! I feel like shouting when yet another writer starts laying into his dad, how mean and strict he was, or how he deserted the family, or taunted his offspring about a weakness at competitive sports. Get over it, I say.)

Reading about Sven's childhood I gathered that the boy Sven was a conventional egghead who couldn't catch a ball and had asthma – like me in fact. Sven, however, waited until he was fifty-one until he addressed these issues. He took up bodybuilding – which, strangely, is quite a favourite with intellectuals as it's non-competitive (except in your own mind as you check out everyone else's muscles), solitary, and ultimately narcissistic (and most intellectuals have definite leanings that way being proud of their brains and independence of thought etc.).

Cheryl said she'd love to come. She added that she had already accepted an invitation to go clubbing with Bradawl on the same evening but she'd meet him later. 'He won't mind if you come too,' she said brightly, but really meaning it.

How naive can you get? But I said to tell him I'd go even though I hate night clubs. Honour demanded it.

Now back to more important matters.

30

To Luxor by first-class train we went – in disguise. 'I have reason to believe we may be followed,' said Dr Ragab, who insisted on dressing as a foreign generalissimo. I was a subaltern and Suleiman the manservant was clad as a monk, much to his distaste. (He refused to wear a cross.) In Luxor we sat on the platform in the blinding noonday sun and waited as the train to Kharga Oasis, *the oasis*, as Herodotus puts it, pulled in, a small saddle-tank steamer with three carriages. Dr Ragab forbade us to board, and at the last moment a group of green-clad dervishes climbed on. 'Your friend's order, I believe,' said Ragab.

We waited a long while in the stifling heat for the next train. Suleiman begged to be allowed to relinquish his monk's disguise and Ragab reluctantly agreed. 'But not you!' he thundered at me. 'But what army is this uniform?' I had asked earlier. 'Paraguay,' snapped Dr Ragab, 'I find it opens a lot of doors when dealing with officious Britishers.' Suleiman grinned at this. He was a graceful Nubian of impeccable manners, always smiling despite regular stinging rebukes from the Doctor.

At Kharga, after Ragab had accomplished mysterious business with a man selling what looked to my eye to be fake Roman amphorae, we clambered into a dusty-looking motor car and were driven the two hundred kilometres to Qasr, the fortified mud-brick town in the oasis of Dakhla. Here, having at last given up the need for disguise, Dr Ragab, dressed in a white suit and panama hat and carrying a rolled black umbrella (despite it last having rained here in 1896), was received like royalty. The *homda*, or headman, insisted on serving us abominable *foul*, broad beans in sauce, whilst slyly angling the conversation towards hunting for buried treasure. Were our own plans of that nature? Dr Ragab airily told all that we sought only the Pillars of Seth. However, everyone in that inward-looking and suspicious place was convinced we were after gold from one of the many lost tombs in the surrounding hills. 'Truth is a marvellous deception in a town full of liars,' remarked the Doctor in German to me.

From now on we would travel by camel. Ragab's was a male, white, about eight years old; his name, Beyoude. The other three, with eyes and head softer and altogether more feminine, were females. The Doctor explained, 'For some reason the Egyptian Bedouin considers the gelding a travesty of creation, whereas the Algerian Berber finds him the most useful of animals. We are stuck therefore with the ill temper of a male and the lower endurance of the female.'

Water was transported in an invention of Ragab's, reminding me of his polymathic nature. 'Your compatriot Rohlfs came here with great riveted iron cans of water, which expanded in the heat and leaked – a disaster. My idea is to use cylinders of copper within saddlebags of waterproof canvas – a leak will be contained and easily observable.'

The canvas bags were like army kitbags. Inside each were two copper cylinders, like giant shell cases, sealed with a screw-top lid. Each cylinder contained fifteen litres, each set of saddlebags sixty – enough water for four men for five days. Beyoude carried a double load – in total we were hauling two hundred and fifty litres – enough for a month. Dr Ragab said the camels would need little water – 'Look at their humps – full of fat – a good hump means a beast can go a month or more without water as long as we find some green vegetation.'

The camel food we brought was corn and sacks of dried birseem, or fodder, a kind of hay, a precaution against finding no tamarisk or desert thorn.

At dawn we mounted our camels and headed south-west out of Dakhla. Ragab explained that we would walk when we were tired of riding and ride when we were tired of walking. Our direction was duly noted by a sleepy *ghaffyr*, or watchman, and certainly reported to the headman and his cronies. It would be assumed that the 'treasure' we sought lay in every direction except the one we were going. Then a young boy came running after us from the town. Dr Ragab gave him two piastres and the boy gabbled his news. It concerned, I was sure, the trivial information that the rest of our supplies, which were awaiting us at the edge of the oasis, would lack flour but not dry bread. Ragab chose to be mysterious and claimed, 'It seems your friend Kasparius passed through yesterday.'

'Why didn't they tell us earlier?'

'He paid them not to.'

I wondered if Dr Ragab was determined to create a more intriguing atmosphere for some teaching purpose.

Whatever he had in mind I did not question him and played along with the idea that we were being stalked by the strange and fanatical Kasparius.

We loaded the last of our food and supplies and the Bedouin boy disappeared at the edge of the oasis. Suleiman now jumped down and led his camel in front, walking briskly. He seemed an experienced camelteer. Dr Ragab, too, was quite expert. He spoke at all times to the large male he was riding with a clucking sound that pacified the great beast. Did he know the language of animals too? He laughed – 'There is nothing to know except how to dominate and how to calm.'

In the heat my trousers felt scratchy and uncomfortable; bulging pockets rubbed my skin. I removed coins, penknife, string, paper and fountain pen to the woven camel bag I'd been assigned for personal equipment. Dr Ragab saw me. 'Put the pen in your top pocket.'

'Why?'

'It won't annoy you there.'

'But I don't need it while we're walking.'

'You never know, you might have to sign some cheques.'

Wearily I clipped my brown pearl Lebouef sleeve-filler to my shirt front pocket.

'Rather nice pen, that,' said Dr Ragab.

After four more hours of camel riding I was sore and bruised in all kinds of new places. Dr Ragab examined his prismatic compass (a gift from Kitchener, he claimed) that he wore on a woven leather string around his neck.

'We have a call to make,' he said, 'to that hill over there.'

31

I gazed in the direction indicated to a distant conical hill with a kind of rock pinnacle on top.

Dr Ragab explained, 'There is a Russian hermit living there. He'll tell us if there have been any Senussi raiders through here recently but you will have to practise *shemell*.'

'Why?'

'Why? Why? Why? It's always why with you Prussians. Why not? That's what I say.'

'I was only asking.'

'Don't. First, it is a common courtesy to call. Second, we may learn something. Third, *you* may learn something, except that is in no way guaranteed.'

I hung my head, beaten in the brassy midday sun. Ragab ignored me and strode ahead, always oblivious to self-pity.

Shemell is a technique for causing one's interlocutor to speak everything that burdens them. Some happen upon the technique by accident but it can be learnt. The point of *shemell* is not to learn someone's inner secrets but to master the state of projecting complete lack of judgement. (Also, as a way of finding out information it is rather inefficient as you hear everything, not just what you want to hear.)

The hill was much further away than I had thought. All distance is distorted in the desert. Quite quickly twilight began to fall. None of us riding anymore, we trudged on and on. As we neared I caught sight of other camel tracks. Dr Ragab nodded his head at them but said nothing.

'Look, there he is!' I followed Suleiman's pointing finger. A figure moved aloft a wooden platform on top of the rocky outcrop. He moved jerkily back and forth, as if at some important task. Then I smelt, carried in the still evening air, the odour of gasoline, very faint. A moment later a great fire lit up on the pinnacle, like an offering to the Gods.

'As if he were guiding us in,' I joked.

'Oh, I'm sure he is,' said Ragab.

We arrived at the hill and saw the considerable habitation wrought by the lone hermit. As well as the platform, he had made, from split palm trunks and sun-bleached tarpaulins, a kind of hangar for what looked like the ruined remains of an aircraft.

'I will not speak,' boomed a voice in French from above.

'He always says that,' said Dr Ragab as we dismounted and stretched our legs. Under my breath I intoned *shemell*.

'I've got something for you,' shouted Dr Ragab up to the flame and billowing black smoke.

'I need nothing,' came the reply. There was a pause. 'I will not speak.'

'It's a fountain pen.'

And then to me in a whisper, 'Give him yours, will you? He has a weakness for them.'

There was a creaking high above us and a section of the overhanging wooden platform began to descend in jerks.

It came faster and faster and hit the sand with a *wumpf*, expelling dust on each side.

Full of the familiar irritation at having been used yet again I climbed onto the square pallet and was winched upwards holding the hairy rope that supported each corner. The smell of goat droppings and smoke increased as I went higher. The view over the ghostly desert was of a moonlit shadowland.

'Take care of your fingers!'

An unsmiling face with a tassel of grey beard at the chin looked at me through the platform hole. It was a red face, concentrating. He turned back to his windlass, a wooden affair, held together by strips of leather.

'I don't want that fountain pen,' he said. 'I haven't even got any ink, apart from pitch and lampblack, which I get from the Bedou.'

I introduced myself but he interrupted, seeing the pen in my top pocket and taking it. He unscrewed the top and smiled at the gold nib.

'So, another professor! One wrote about me in Trieste, an Italian. We had a German here the other day too. That's right, sit there.'

He indicated a plank resting across two old camel saddles. Then he dropped the pallet again for Ragab and as he wound he talked.

'See my fire, did you? I like to make it visible for miles. The people round here like it. They like to know I'm up here on my own.'

When Dr Ragab arrived and was seated the hermit looked at me. 'You look funny, you do.'

To project no judgement you have to imagine you are looking at the back of the person's head as they talk to you.

'I should say I don't like chatting with just anyone,' he added.

There was a long silence. I sank my centre down as low as it could go and imagined my upper body as a mere skeleton made of transparent bones.

'How long will you stay?' he asked eventually.

'Not long.'

'I don't let anyone stay overnight. Not right.'

'We'll be gone very soon.'

'You can stay a bit. I'm not unfriendly. Just not too long.'

'We'll be off very shortly.'

'You could stay but only if I asked permission of the angels.'

'Don't trouble them, please,' said Dr Ragab. 'Not on our account.'

The hermit looked scornful. 'You can't trouble an angel. It doesn't work like that.'

Neither of us spoke and after searching the horizon, perhaps for an emissary of the heavens, the hermit sighed and then he started. 'It was Mr Ionides who put me up to this, yes he changed my life all right, a good man, a very good-hearted man. He lives in the Levant and visits once a year with his family. He comes by camel like you did. Makes a picnic of it though I won't have children up here, same reason that I never became a salesman. My family were all hussars in Russia. We have our traditions. Women and children! I get three or four people a week out here, sometimes less. There are people in Moscow who see less folk than me. Sometimes I tell them to clear off, don't let down the lifter. Can't be bothered with all the complaints. Bedou always complaining how their neighbour's a rotten thief. I'm not here as a judge, I say. One fellow wanted me to go and help get his wife back from another tribe. I sent him off with a flea in his ear!

'They understand now that I don't come down. That's all part of it. If I started coming down they'd lose their respect. I know that. As it is they do my bidding pretty well. I shout down to them when they get too close to the plane, that's my only concern, that they try to steal something off it to make a saddle or a knife blade.'

I glimpsed the edge of a canvas-covered wing down below. He really did have an aeroplane parked out here.

'I have one fellow who comes and turns over the engine at each full moon and new moon. They like to do it at night and hear the noise. The kids don't like the noise but the old ones do. He runs the engines at low revs for a few minutes, ten perhaps, until they warm up, and that's it. He can clean a carburettor. Mr Ionides left him kerosene for that. It's all worked out.'

'But why?' I had to ask.

'It's all part of it. My agreement with Mr Ionides.'

'What sort of agreement?'

'It doesn't matter now, but at first I was a little reluctant shall we say. I wanted to know when my time was up that I could leave on the dot like a tram.' He tittered and then rubbed his rimmed eyes.

'When your time is up? When's that?' I asked.

'Oh, I should say February 12th 1952. If I'm still around.'

We sat in silence for a while contemplating the thought of spending more than two decades on this rough platform of palm wood.

'Yes, twenty-seven more years,' said the hermit and he started to weep.

'Oh, it's not what you think.' He rubbed his eyes. 'I just start weeping these days for no reason. On account of the little children,' he said in a peculiar voice perhaps intended to be funny.

Dr Ragab said, 'Have you been getting the mare's milk recently? You used to enjoy that. You made it into a kind of kvass, didn't you?'

The hermit was looking far out over the desert, rubbing his eyes. 'That fellow robbed me. It doesn't matter. They wanted me to put a curse on him but I didn't, though I could and I should think it would work out here too.' He looked at us defiantly.

'I'll fly out of here one day,' he said, 'they all know it.'

'Of course you will,' said Dr Ragab smoothly.

'I've been thinking a lot about angels recently,' said the hermit. 'There are two kinds that I know of – guardian angels that keep you out of trouble and messenger angels that tell you things.'

'What sort of things?' I asked.

The hermit looked at me as if I was stupid then he turned to Dr Ragab. 'Aren't teaching the professors much these days, are they?' My ears burned even though I knew he was just an ignorant fellow. I forced myself to 'look' at the back of his head.

'It was Mr Ionides that saw a way through it for me. We were in Turkey after the war and it was a pitiable state we lived in. He gave me hope and reminded me how no man can live without his God. NO MAN CAN LIVE WITHOUT HIS GOD!' he shouted out to the desert night sky.

'Mr Ionides had me going back to church. It was like water to me after a drought. I needed that water. I wasn't going to get through life without it. You realize you aren't so special after all and everyone else is a fool or a thief, except a few of them like Mr Ionides. Then he came up with his plan and I saw that it was the answer, it worked for both of us, you see.'

I was beginning to get the picture. 'Where will you live after . . . this?'

'Oh, that's all taken care of, just like my wife is taken care of, though she hardly knows it, poor dear. That was part of it, that's my reward isn't it, though I see it more like an acknowledgement. The church was built on a rock and men *must* pay for it.'

The hermit then spoke lengthily about the cures and contagions of the people around, he mentioned the magic they believed in that he hoped to rid them of and in the same breath spoke of the curses he could rain down on anyone who betrayed him. There were no Senussi raiders about or so he had heard.

'Even so you should stay till dawn,' he said, 'lot of snakes around here.'

'We really should be going.'

'Scorpions too. Snakes and scorpions. Don't want the professor getting bit.'

'I've already been bitten by a cobra,' I said.

The hermit ignored me. 'Had a fellow through here yesterday. He wouldn't stay either. Also German. Also a professor by the look of him. Head shaped like a turnip. Gave me this.'

It was a manual of dervish exercises in Arabic.

'Can't read it but I like the pattern the writing makes.'

We eventually took leave of the hermit some hours before sunrise. I was still annoyed about my pen.

Ragab ignored my obvious irritation. 'It seems that your friend Kasparius precedes us.'

'I noticed that too. The turnip-headed German.'

'Precisely.'

'Were those his tracks we saw earlier?'

'Yes. He's going the direct route, which is a little more risky.'

We rode on through the desert. When the hill was far behind there came an odd echoey cough and then the unmistakable roar of two engines. In the still of dawn the vibrating sound seemed very close, pummelling the air, following us for miles.

'Does Mr Ionides actually *pay* him to be a hermit?'

'Yes.'

I could feel a sudden rage building up inside. The desert climate worsened any irritation, I knew that. I took a deep breath, or whatever one does when later it *feels* as though one took a deep breath . . . 'So why the hell don't you tell him he's wasting his time? That sitting up there is just a way of providing entertainment for bored Bedouins? That the age of hermits passed fifteen hundred years ago?

That he is mortgaging his present for some idiotic future security?'

Dr Ragab, far from being insulted, looked rather pleased. 'Why didn't you tell him yourself? It's not really our Eastern style to go at things head-on, we're far too sly for that.' He rode on, unconcerned.

We did not speak for a long time. For a while I thought I could still hear the hermit's engine but it was just the desert wind; light and hardly noticeable, at the very edge of audition.

Had my *shemell* really been the cause of the hermit's loquaciousness or would he have talked anyway? Something had happened, but what exactly was hard to say. I saw then the impossibility of any scientist or academic ever approaching the Universal Language, it was far too elusive.

The sun climbed higher and I could feel its warmth. I felt calmer now and asked the Doctor if he had ever met Mr Ionides.

'Twice.'

'What's he like?'

Dr Ragab thought for a moment. 'A charming hypocrite.'

32

We carried on across a belt of sand dunes, dismounting so that the camels could climb the treacherous slip face more easily. It was like ascending the tumbling sand in an hourglass.

Dr Ragab consulted the map then his compass. He pointed towards a shimmering plain of flat sand. 'We go north,' he pronounced.

Underfoot (I was now walking and leading my camel as a relief from the agony of riding) I saw the fractured remains of flint tools and pieces of hand-made pottery. Dr Ragab pointed to a pile of three flat stones resting on a large weather-beaten rock. 'That "alem" is older than the pyramids,' he said. I was tempted to knock it down, but, of course, did not.

I have recently been asking myself: What was in it for Dr Ragab? Why did he expend so much effort in trying to teach me? Once I asked him.

'There is a requirement,' he said, 'that to move forward, up the spiral staircase so to speak, one must fill the space left empty.'

I felt rather pleased with this answer. Here, almost *before* I registered my pride, he added, with a deftness which has something to do with coincidence and is, on reflection, more magical than any of the 'magic' he practised, 'Actually almost anyone will do to fill that space.'

Our desert journey wound on towards our fabulous destination. I knew that then I would be in possession of all I sought. The wisdom of the ancients, all truth of real value, the knowledge set down to survive the flood. Of course I told myself I'd probably fail in some way, that something would harm or hinder us – but I didn't believe it.

33

We came now upon the edge of the Great Sand Sea. Years before, the German explorer Rohlfs had been here and almost perished. As the camels stumbled down the side of a huge dune a sudden booming sound began. Then another sound started up, one quite extraordinary. A tuneful screech is the best I can do to describe it, musical, yet betraying its origin in the movement of dry sand grain over dry sand grain. Dr Ragab pointed and I could see the slippage, as the crest of the dune rode down its own ridge. Then another dune began to tune up and then the one behind that. All of a sudden I was surrounded by the singing sands, each note different, yet harshly complimentary, the music rising and falling to no pattern, gradually fading. I found myself listening harder, as if vainly trying to follow that last disappearing sound to its destination, and then it was silent again with only the wind sounding in my ears.

Dr Ragab spoke of the history of this wadi, a shallow valley that ran along a winding line of tamarisk bushes half buried in sand. It had long been known as a source of buried treasure since the time of Joseph and the Pharaohs. Ibn Tufail mentions the many Arab expeditions to find the hidden gold of the place and even today the wandering Bedouin with their camels and dogs will select a spot because of a shadow or an oddly shaped boulder and begin to dig slowly at first and then madly, shouting to their family and to God, sure that they have found the treasure at last.

Up above two falcons were mewing against the brilliant blue of the sky. Suleiman pointed to a low rocky outcrop with sand creeping up its sides. At the outcrop I felt something, as if this place had been previously inhabited. I was beginning to get a sense of place in the desert, a certain feeling that we were on a path trod before, many times. People leave their imprint. When I remarked on this to Dr Ragab he said, 'What – are you some kind of dog now, sniffing the footprints of long-departed men?'

Suleiman gave a shout and waved us to a hole in the wall of the outcrop, about head height. Inside, on a bed of sand, were three falcon eggs. Suleiman was looking around as I was, expectant. Whatever Ragab said, I sensed something about that place. Rounding a corner, I saw that at the foot of the outcrop large flat stones as big as car wheels had been leant against the overhanging rock, effectively sealing it off. Suleiman and I dropped to our knees and pulled the slabs away to reveal a cave with a sand floor sloping away.

'We need to dig,' I said. 'Get the spades.'

Dr Ragab looked down at us as we shovelled away and consulted his gold hunter watch. 'We haven't got all day, you know, to waste on idle treasure hunts.'

I squinted up at him, my face smeared with sweat and sand.

'I grant you it's a new discovery,' he said equably. 'But of what?'

‘I think it is most likely a nomad’s tomb,’ I said.

‘Perhaps.’

Suleiman crawled in and wrinkled up his nose. ‘There’s something dead in here, all right,’ he said.

I could smell nothing. Then I saw the femur wrapped in linen dark with age. Suleiman uncovered the head and torso, skin stretched in perfect dryness into the rictus of a ghastly smile. The eyes were shut, the brown brow wrinkled, the lips a sort of rind covering blackened teeth.

Dr Ragab, despite his earlier disdain, now grew enthusiastic, dropping to his knees to help us clear more sand.

Suleiman said he was convinced there was treasure and dug here and there in an increasing frenzy. Dr Ragab held up his hand. ‘The only treasure is on this man’s back. Have a closer look.’ I perused the hardened skin, shrunk around the protruding vertebrae in a dusty grey ridge. I saw faint blue dots in five places.

‘These?’

‘Yes. Those dots correspond to a series of graduated inner perspectives that can be awakened by certain exercises or certain experiences. This body is six thousand years old or more; they knew more than most know now.’ I bowed my head while Suleiman sifted through the sand still absentmindedly feeling for gold.

34

We continued for days. Increasingly I preferred walking alongside my camel in the shade to riding. I dwelt on the past, my missed opportunities. I thought often of little Hagar, for what reason I did not know. At long last we halted between dunes of white sand, brilliantly lit by the sun. 'There is our destination,' said Dr Ragab, indicating with his chin a rise in the far, far distance.

We started to walk towards this hill or small mountain but it soon disappeared from view as we descended into a low lying section of the sands. We passed a group of *yardangs* or mud lions, their strange shape reminiscent of the sphinx. Unlike the sphinx, though, these were naturally carved by the wind from a blunt mesa of soft shale. As we walked, our light linen suits soaked with sweat and our feet sinking with each step, Dr Ragab talked of the sun and the desire of the man lost in the desert to constantly look at it, to seek it out, until, by over-exposure, he becomes blind.

I remember listening to this advice and heavily walking on. I drew ahead. Suleiman was leading the front camel and the others followed it, laden with packs. It was very hot but every scrap of sweat was evaporating. I was deep in my thoughts and we were past the mud lions and I could again see the mountain, which shimmered like a mirage, though Ragab assured me it was not a mirage. Head down I decided to walk without looking so that I could avoid the painful sense of making no progress.

When I looked up I saw that I was alone. The mud lions lay behind me, far distant. The mountain lay ahead. Of Dr Ragab there was no sign. How could I have lost him? I looked towards the place where I imagined him to be but I could see nothing. I turned and ran back, my canvas and rubber boots sloppy on my feet. Examining my tracks I saw none but my own. I bent over, heaving dry breath. Running had been very stupid. I reached down and touched the sand. It was as hot as a piece of glowing charcoal. The sun. It was high above me, burning a white hole in the sky. I stared upwards at it, checking its position. I did it again, a moment later.

Then it struck me that I was doing exactly what Dr Ragab had advised against, mere minutes after instruction. Was I stupid? I determined to walk, head down, to the mountain and shelter in whatever shade there was to be had.

For some reason though I looked up before I reached my destination. All around me the horizon was distorted into a lake-like mirage. The hills looked like islands. I saw a mirror flash of light in the distance. The light flashed again, perhaps, a little nearer. Then a comma of black, a distinct shape hovering it seemed came towards me. It shimmered, disappearing now and then behind the shallow dunes, and then reappearing more closely. Then without warning this black shape became Dr Ragab riding full pelt on his camel, the bags lifting at the back with each galloping step.

He shouted from a distance: 'Are you all right? Are you all right, my boy?' He was anxious and unnerved. My tongue and upper palate stuck together. I could only nod.

'I bent down to tie my shoelace and you were gone,' he explained. 'You must have disappeared between dunes.' Now he was laughing with relief. He hugged me across the back, still holding the camel rope in his hand, and such was the genuine warmth I lost my inhibition to speak. My tone, however, was forlorn.

'Weren't you teaching me a lesson about not looking at the sun?' I said.

He grinned and shook his head, 'Not at all. I made a mistake. I'm allowed some time off, aren't I?'

The next day we came across Senussi tracks. The Senussi, a fearsome Muslim order, had destroyed the east–west camel routes of the previous century, preferring poverty to allowing others through their lands. If caught we would be treated as spies. Suleiman on his knees explained there had been twenty camels this way only a day or so earlier. He looked enquiringly at Dr Ragab, who said nothing.

35

It was then a strange thing happened, which averted disaster I now think. We were resting in the shade of one of many convenient conical hills that dotted this part of the desert. The tops were capped with harder limestone that protected the base from being eroded. Dr Ragab, as he often did, wandered away in his panama hat, stooping from time to time to pick up rocks (he already had a saddlebag full of fine Palaeolithic burins and scrapers). I must have dozed off for a second or two because Suleiman awoke me by shaking my sleeve in panic. 'Look,' he whispered.

Perhaps a mile away a long line of camels appeared. Too far away to make out the details one thing was clear: *they were walking right into the path of the doctor*. Who stood there, in a white hat with a red neckerchief, quite still but utterly visible for miles around. If the Senussi found us we could expect no quarter. Suleiman drew his finger across his throat.

Any minute now they would fall upon Dr Ragab with their scimitars and ancient matchlock rifles. I felt utterly helpless, able to do nothing from this distance. We could not shout as that would just alert them quicker. All we could do was wait, a horrible feeling. One of our camels raised its head from the sand where it lay and Suleiman whispered to it to stay down. I hardly breathed.

Moving quite quickly, the line of raiders crossed in front of us. They could not miss him. I reached for the binoculars but Suleiman shook his head and nodded towards the sun – a flash of light might give us away.

I then ignobly wished that Dr Ragab would pretend he was alone and somehow the Senussi would leave Suleiman and me – but I knew this was impossible.

All this time the Doctor stood still. He had seen them too, no doubt. I waited for the blood-curdling shrieks and cries the Senussi made when they attacked. Every malign thought I had ever directed against Dr Ragab I regretted. I loved him and could not bear to see him killed.

I scanned again the line of raiders, now almost upon him. Surely now they would charge.

I looked back from the raiders to poor Dr Ragab. He was not there. The ground was flat. There was nowhere to hide. He had simply disappeared. I looked at Suleiman who looked as stunned as I was. Dr Ragab had become invisible.

Yes: one minute there, the next gone. Suleiman muttered, 'He has vanished! He is a jinn!'

Of course I blamed the heat, which was intense, the light, which was blinding – all these things had *confused my senses*. Yet the evidence was there: I had seen it. The man had disappeared. But I still did not believe what I had seen.

Nevertheless, when I raised my eyes and shaded them against the brilliant splintering light of the sun I had every reason to trust what I saw. The camel train had passed. The empty desert stretched between two conical hills and away to a distant horizon. Minutes which seemed like hours later, a shimmering, like a mirage walking into existence, Dr Ragab appeared in front of us, quite unconcerned.

Neither Suleiman nor I spoke as he approached. 'Did you see those rascals?' Ragab asked. 'They definitely had trouble on their minds. I was reminded of that joke when a man sees some soldiers and hides, and when they come over and ask what he's up to he replies, "It's a bit tricky but I'm here because you're here . . . and you're here because I'm here."'

We continued staring at him.

'Naturally I didn't want to explain all this to those bandits so I made myself invisible.'

Suleiman, who had seen many strange things whilst in the Doctor's employ, began reciting a verse of the Koran, hurriedly, as if his life depended on it.

'It's actually rather easy,' the Doctor said. 'Just imagine you are nothing, a mere dot. Less than a dot. You've got an active imagination,' he said to me, 'you'd probably be quite good at it.'

I knew enough not to ask more. I had seen him do it. I had seen a man make himself invisible and I believed.

An hour later we had another shock. Suleiman was adjusting the camel loads when one saddle slid down. I went to help with the heavy water containers but they were suspiciously light. Both had been cracked, probably by the camel lying sideways on them, and the water had evaporated away through tiny holes worn in the canvas. Despite his patent system having supremely failed, Ragab was unabashed. Suleiman then discovered two more cylinders had leaked. We had enough water for another day and a half at most.

'Don't give up yet,' Dr Ragab joked to our blank faces, 'we're only ninety kilometres from the nearest well.'

We lay up in the shade of a rock until it grew cool enough to move. 'For those of you still interested,' said Dr Ragab in a conversational tone, 'we're leaning against the Pillar of Seth.'

'But it's a rock, not a pillar!' I protested.

'Rock, pillar – in ancient translations they often mean the same. Look at the hieroglyphics.'

Carved deep into the limestone, just above head height, was a circle with radiating lines. The circle was really a tight spiral. At the end of each extending line was an eye, and each one also contained a spiral.

It reminded me of the sun frieze found at Tel el-Amarna, the city built by Akhnaten. I said as much and Dr Ragab nodded. 'You are on the right lines. The sun, and at the end of each ray, another eye.'

'Another?'

'The spiralling effect also indicates an eye. An observing eye.'

'That is also the sun?'

'That's it. In one sense that is the entire wisdom of mankind. Everything we know. Everything we will ever know.' He raised his eyebrows with a touch of irony.

'I told you coming here would do no good.'

I was outraged and disgusted at this practical joke, as I saw it. Ragab had gone too far. We could have died, and of course we still could die, messing about looking at Stone Age graffiti! I barely studied the engraved rocks which seemed to fascinate Suleiman; I wanted no part of this silly charade. I just fumed in the stifling heat and said nothing.

'What fun we're having, but I suppose we should be going.' Dr Ragab had the awful cheerfulness he always affected whenever anyone was in a black mood.

Meanwhile I was feeling rather chilly waiting in the pouring rain for Cheryl at the entrance of Hyde Park Corner Tube. She was not late but I was early. I also had wet feet. Earlier, realizing I ought to dress smartly, I'd put on my black shoes that need resoling. Hurrying through the rain I had successfully managed to avoid five or six puddles, then, just as I approached Ealing station, I'd stepped hard on a loose paving slab that squirted water through the sole, soaking my sock.

I stood watching the rain drip like liquid icicles. Every few minutes I checked my watch, smearing away the odd drip of rain. It soon became imperative to leave or else I would be late. I phoned from a callbox Cheryl's house and she answered saying she was glad I rang because she'd burnt her hand on her Mig welder and had been to the hospital but it was OK now, thanks for asking, no, really OK, and she was sorry she'd be missing Sven but she'd meet me afterwards outside the Ministry of Sound (where Richard Bradawl commanded VIP status). If that was OK? It was OK.

I hurried on alone towards the light blue flag of the Swedish Embassy, which flapped against the twilit sky. Wet with a wet foot I was ushered through the townhouse splendour of the reception. Filipino-looking men and women brought round drinks and canapés with a Swedish bent, mainly to do with roll-mop herrings. I surveyed the crowd – mostly elderly and foreign, too well dressed to be from London. There was free white wine and I made the most of it, taking one in with me to the reading.

Sven was short and plump, despite all the bodybuilding. He had a grey closely cropped beard, a bald head, and was dressed entirely in black, the serious writer's favourite uniform. What is it with black? Surely black is the colour of mourning? What was Sven mourning? The death of the novel?

Black hides bulges. Writers, apart from Burroughs and Beckett, always get fat and shapeless owing to so much time sitting in front of a typewriter or keyboard. Salman's big bum, one publisher told me, is a great advert against the writer's life.

Black removes the need to choose. Writers are bad at making real-world choices.

Black is cheap. You should see how many market-stall black T-shirts you can get for ten pounds.

But above all black is serious, pessimistic, cool, and not what people who work in offices wear.

Sven wore a black shirt and a foreign correspondent's jacket, the kind with zips and pockets, except it was black, even the zips were black, black and chunky. He wore black trousers, a little tight, and tiny black shiny Chelsea boots in good shape not all beat up like some writers affect to wear.

Just showing in the 'V' of his ironed black shirt was a black T-shirt worn underneath.

His socks were probably white – I just suspected that for some reason.

Even though he looked like a black dwarf Sven was my favourite living writer because of his magnum opus: *A Short*

History of Bunkers. Everything Sven wrote, or at least everything of his that has been translated from the Swedish, was a 'short history of something or other'. Sven had an elaborate intellectual defence against the need for long histories, but one suspected the real reason was he couldn't be arsed.

And anyway I preferred short books.

Bunkers was a work of research genius. The pages were full of both bunker plans and photos as well as text written in numbered paragraphs that could be linked non-chronologically even though the book was set out in chronological order. These links showed the way Sven had unearthed a real history of bunkers as the cause of conflict – the Maginot Line for example and the trenches of World War I and the defensive line of the Republicans in the Spanish Civil War. Not to mention Stalingrad, in which an entire city became a bunker.

Sven and I, I've always, perhaps rather lazily, thought, operate on a similar wavelength. (I've even got a few black clothes myself.) He gave a short reading which was OK, good in fact, since ninety-five per cent of all writers reading their work bore me rigid. Writers mistakenly think everyone loves their book as much as they do and read for far too long. And far too quietly. Sven was bearably short and tolerably loud. A good performance given that English is his third language (he's got five). Then the questions started.

The questions came mainly from Swedish sycophants resident in the UK. Sven deliberated on even the most banal as if he was passing a religious judgement. He was, I sadly realized, truly pompous. One questioner, a very well-dressed man of about sixty, he looked like a banker, asked politely (it was all in English out of deference to the host nation, and because they all could),

'Mr Marquist, should we be optimistic or generally pessimistic about the future?'

This was delivered with the full force of 'the future', meaning the future of life on this planet.

Instead of answering, 'How should I know?' Sven stroked his beard and said, 'Optimism, pessimism – these are difficult terms.'

No they're not. What got me was his complacent assumption that these questions should be asked of him. He fully believed that he was a 'thinker' of our time, a guru with the answers, at least for well-fed Swedes with time on their hands in London. But still I was willing to give him the benefit of the doubt. I blamed the situation not the man.

I stuck up my hand. 'Mr Marquist, have you ever been injured bodybuilding?'

He laughed condescendingly. The audience joined in. Far from it being the clever antidote to too much hot air, my comment was perceived as naively stupid. Couldn't Sven see I was a believer, a supporter?

He couldn't.

Pessimism and optimism became a kind of theme in his answers (except to my question, which he brushed aside with a brief 'No.'). I thought of Wittgenstein's comment, 'What could be more different than a sad and happy man's vision of the world?' That made more sense than Sven's equivocation. In the end, aided by more agreeable laughter, he announced he was pessimistically optimistic about the future.

What did that mean except as an avowal to keep wearing black?

Sven's books are widely distributed and read all over the world. Hertwig's book has been read by very few. I prefer

Hertwig. Back outside, full of white wine, rained on and still with a damp foot, I headed by Tube towards the Ministry of Sound. When I was almost there, the station before the right stop, I got off the train and crossed to the other side of the platform. A train going the other way pulled in and I got on. There were plenty of seats and I started to read again.

36

As night fell we stumbled on in a dispirited line, Dr Ragab at the lead. We kept one *guerba* of water refilled from the dwindling supplies and munched on a handful of dates. He handed those out at midnight beneath a brilliant carpet of stars. Two hours later, not one star was visible but it was strangely light and the wind was rising. Dr Ragab remained cheerful but Suleiman muttered about the *khamsin*, the fifty days of bad weather in late March and April. The wind quickly grew worse and even, for a few minutes, a light rain fell. That is good, said Suleiman, for it will lay the dust.

But it did not.

There are two kinds of storm in the desert. The sandstorm and the dust storm. A sandstorm is relatively benign. Sand, being heavy, can only rise two or so metres above the ground. If you can climb a rock in a sandstorm you can look out over a sea, a fog of whipping sand particles. Sometimes even being on a camel is enough to raise you above it.

A dust storm is much worse. Dust penetrates through the headscarf around your face (though it will always keep sand particles out). Dust storms are choking and hot. They can go on for days and in their centre it can be a suffocating inferno with a temperature of over forty-five degrees.

The wind howled, the dust blew – the *khamsin* had arrived in full gale force. Dr Ragab, head bowed and wrapped like a mummy, tied a rope from his waist to mine and then to Suleiman, who led the train of camels. Visibility was less than three metres. All around us was a superheated fog. My hands were whipped raw by the billowing hot dust. Dr Ragab navigated from the front using his prismatic compass.

If we had had sufficient water perhaps we would have tried to rest. All of us knew, however, that this was night, despite the heat, and we had to make the most of it. By day it would be even hotter. Even so, as each minute passed more moisture was sucked from our already dry skins. We pressed on while we could still walk.

My ears were full of dust, impairing my hearing. I could feel Suleiman dragging on my rope as he stumbled along behind me, slowing us all up. On and on we trudged into the blinding winds.

The fog grew lighter – that was the only indication of dawn. Then, as the day progressed, I saw a silver coin, which was the sun, almost obscured by dust. The day became hotter and hotter and the winds grew worse. We could hardly breathe, and when we did, the air stung and burned.

Dr Ragab allowed each only a sip of water, using the cap from the binoculars to dish out a precise ration. 'More! I need more!' roared Suleiman, his dark eyes rimmed with red. The man was losing his mind, I could see.

We found a shallow pit to sit out the worst of the midday heat. Suleiman was panting like a dog. It was most dispiriting. When he wasn't panting he was praying, all kinds of scraps of prayer and verses from the Koran.

Just when I thought that Suleiman was right and all was lost, Dr Ragab perked up. 'What you fellows need is a good *dirty* story.' Suleiman's prayers halted then began again a little more quietly.

'Oh, do stop that,' said Ragab, 'you're not dead yet.' Suleiman stopped.

37

'A certain man,' said Dr Ragab, 'was an insatiable lover of fair women, and he spent and spent his wealth upon them until he was poor and reduced to begging for hard bread in the daily marketplace. His clothes were ragged and his sandals torn and he walked with little care for anyone or anything. One day he brushed against the door of a house and caught his hand on an iron nail sticking from the door post. It tore the flesh of his finger and he cried out. Then he wiped away the blood and bound it up with a piece of palm leaf he found in the gutter.

'"I deserve some luxury after such a misfortune," he thought and he hurried towards the nearby door of a *hammam*, a public bath. He looked in and saw the place was clean and empty so he took his clothes off and sitting next to a pool with a fountain in the middle he poured jug after jug of water over his head.

'He began to feel pleasantly tired. Then he went into the room with the large cistern of cold water and seeing no one there he went over to a quiet corner and took out a small piece of hashish he had kept for a while in the waist of his robe. After a while the emanations of the drug rose to his brain and he rolled over onto the marble floor, whose pattern he noticed was veined in red like the eye of a madman.

'In his mind he saw that a great lord was shampooing his hair and two slaves attended him. "This must be a mistake," he thought, for though he was already fuddled by the effects of the drug, he was not yet completely insensible. Then in his fancy he imagined the bathman saying to him, "O master, it is time for thy visit to the palace for today it is thy turn of service." '

At this point Dr Ragab broke off and explained that hashish has the effect of exciting the imagination, and of making one almost immune to heat. 'It is taken by all the stokers,' he said, 'as they come through the Suez Canal. Only a man who has taken hashish can withstand the combined heat of the boilers and the Sinai Desert.' Then he returned to his tale.

'The deluded man believed he was being led to the palace and there he was installed in the private rooms of the great prince. The rooms were full of fruits and flowers and on an ebony stool he was seated and the bathman again washed him and rubbed him with oils scented with attar of roses, persimmon and musk. "Now, O great lord and master, we will leave you," said the bathman, and he left with the two slaves.

'Once he was alone the man arose, removed the cloth from around his middle and laughed until it hurt. "What must be wrong with them that they think I am a prince or a great wazir? They are happily blundering now, but in an hour or so they'll come to their senses and fall to kicking and cuffing me with blows."

'There was then a knock at the door and a small white slave and a great eunuch did enter, carrying a pair of *kubkab*, or bath clogs, and three silken cloths. They tied one cloth around his head, another around his chest and a third around his middle. Then two more eunuchs lifted him upon a sedan chair and carried him to a room with a luxurious divan upon which lay a delightful slave girl naked save for seven diaphanous silks around her curved body.

'The eunuchs left and the man began to kiss and fondle the slave girl, who was most eager to please. He sat between her legs and taking his manhood strongly in his hand he began to tease and tantalize the slave girl's pudendum.'

Dr Ragab motioned with his hand the action involved and Suleiman tittered. 'The slave girl opened her legs wide and he pushed himself towards her when loud in his ear he heard, "Wake up, you vagabond. We are due to open and you are still asleep." He opened his eyes and found himself surrounded by a crowd of laughing people.

'The people were laughing and laughing and the man looked down whereupon he saw that his penis was fully erect and exposed. "You should be ashamed," they shouted, "sleeping stark naked with a stiff standing tool!" The man awoke fully from his dream and complained as their cuffs and blows fell upon him, "At least you could have waited until I put it in!" '

Dr Ragab led us in a muted round of dry laughter. He allowed us another binocular cap of water and I retied my scarf. The cloth still snapped in the wind, but was it my imagination or had the gale lessened? We marched on and on – I checked my watch but it had stopped, choked on dust. The sand underfoot gave way to ground that was flat and gravelly, hard on the soles, but Ragab was jubilant, announcing that we had reached the plains south of Dakhla. 'We're home, my boys, home!' But we were not. Hour after hour we dragged our carcases, urged on by Ragabian advice ('On a flat surface even a sick man can walk indefinitely', 'Count your steps, it'll make walking almost too easy'). The wind blew just as strongly, yet I could now see at least half a kilometre ahead. We were out of the storm's centre but this hardly registered. Every emotion was turned off, all energy desperately needed for moving forward. My skin felt thickened, numb from the assault of wind-driven sand. My throat seemed blocked by a giant lump, my legs puppetlike and weak and still we walked, into another night. Before daybreak, stumbling with cracked lips, we arrived at Bir Yusef, a pool of clear water between two giant rocks, water reflecting the moon. Drinking only a sip at a time, we all of us gave thanks for our lives.

The phone rang. I didn't want to answer but I did. Cheryl. The news was, objectively speaking, good, but still semi-disquieting. They'd danced the night away but nothing more. This was implied but not stated. I didn't care. I knew not and cared not whether Dirty Dick had triumphed with his silvered shiv. Except I did. It was time to forget Cheryl, so of course I spent a lot of time thinking about her. Odd stuff.

I remember how sometimes Cheryl would gasp as she switched on a light and say, 'Isn't electricity amazing!'

But isn't everything amazing when you're in that mood? Which is a great mood to be in but you never are for long.

I thought of her getting up early to go to her two jobs (art therapy is a precarious profession) or off to her group studio (old car dealership in Leytonstone squatted by conceptual artists in the nineties) where she uses her Mig welder to make those gigantic steel women with long legs and short bodies, angular space-age Barbie dolls from the robot planet Zorg.

I thought about a previous low point in our relationship that actually became a turning point, a kind of low turning point, rather, in Cardiff during a pouring rain storm as I gouged skin off my knuckles trying to re-assemble robot spider woman gives birth ('deliverance' was the real title). We were outside in a public park completely drenched and discovering that it is much, much easier to take a robot spider woman apart than to bolt the fucking thing together again. I was up in the top branches (it was as huge as a metal tree) and swearing at the six-inch gap between two limbs that would not connect. I knew we would have to unbolt the whole thing and do it in a different order to close that gap.

I looked at Cheryl as she proffered a huge adjustable wrench, her concerned eager face, her tiny nose red in the driving rain.

'Why can't you make small sculptures? Ornaments? Maquettes? Why the fuck does everything have to be so big?'

Cheryl simply smiled. I thought about that smile, on and off, quite a lot.

38

On the train back to Cairo I felt inexplicably homesick. I made up my mind to tell Ragab my father was ill and needed visiting. I could not forget the idiotic charade of Seth's 'Pillar'. It depressed me, this everyday acceptance of fraud. This insufferable Easternness I kept calling it, this not knowing where you were or what was what or who was who.

A day after thinking up my excuse I received a letter from my mother. My father had fallen and fractured two vertebrae in his neck. The science of coincidence was working against me. He was not dead. The spinal cord was unharmed. However a bruise on his arm had refused to heal and now he was dangerously ill and calling for me, my mother wrote, and I knew from the quality of what was unsaid, the weight of her words, how the paper had been punctured at one point by the point of the pen, I understood from that he was dying. I looked again at the narrowing then widening gaps between the words, slight, but noticeable as she signed her name, holding the nib down too hard so that in release it sprang forward and flung its small load of ink. I read my mother's suffering into that letter, though the content was bland enough: 'he would be very pleased to see you', 'the doctor has high hopes', 'he is fixing that clock in your old room.'

I was surprised that Dr Ragab wasn't more considerate. He looked annoyed when I told him and immediately pestered me to know how long I would be away. 'I can't possibly say,' I said haughtily, attempting to imitate his own manner. It failed miserably. He simply gave me a look that seemed on the verge of insulting laughter.

There was a visitor that day, a Hungarian aristocrat who wanted to interest Dr Ragab in a scheme to precipitate rain from clouds seeded with silver nitrate. Ragab spoke to him about the human capacity for doing unintentional damage. He addressed all his comments to the eager Hungarian, a common technique of his, yet I was sure they were intended for me.

'Imagine,' pontificated Ragab in a leisurely tone, 'that you have a household pest – rats, termites, wasps or whatever; imagine, too, that by some strange happenstance you could teach a termite to create, not destroy. Yet since the termite has an immense capacity for doing damage one's first efforts would be necessarily directed not at teaching the best and most promising termites but at diverting those with the greatest capacity to do harm.'

I could not let this lie without comment. 'What if those with the most capacity to do harm were also the most promising?'

Ragab smiled as if at a dim but eager child. 'Look at the condition of this world and ask yourself *is that really likely*.'

My homesickness and concern for my father alternated with a dread of leaving. I thought of how little I had learned. Anxious to profitably fill whatever time I had left I asked Dr Ragab how he had become invisible. 'I told you it is actually rather easy,' he said.

'But how?'

'As with anything – start small, work up to what you want to do, be prepared to let go of what you've learnt to make the leap, that cannot be explained except poorly in words, to the level where the skill operates.'

I nodded hesitantly.

'You really have to be spoon-fed, don't you? Try and get into the Khedival club wearing native costume – tell yourself you expect to be stopped but at the same time *imagine* yourself invisible.'

'But isn't there some special phrase I need to say?'

'Yes, but it won't work until you have an idea of where you are going. You have to start small. Remember there is a continuum from the way the world really is to its exploitation by the Universal Language. You must see the way the world really is first.'

I did as he suggested. I understood that what I could learn from self-observation would be the clue that would allow me to really be invisible. At this stage, the Doctor implied, I had to be content with being *unperceived as anything of significance*. First I knew not to look at the guard. Ragab had mentioned in passing that every living creature knows when it is being observed even through a glass window. How? Because light is the carrier wave for other, subtler, undetectable – by science – information.

At the same time as not looking I imagined myself transparent; I visualized the guard seeing the brick wall of the entrance through my body. I shrank my essence, centre, sense of self, to a dot, a hovering full stop. All this got me a few feet further than if I'd walked up to the desk normally.

Dr Ragab laughed when I told him of my endeavours. 'Try this next time: tell yourself you are the British Ambassador, Sir Miles Lampton no less. You know that rather endearing way he walks. Become him in your mind as you stroll through the gates. This, by the way, is the essence of disguise, making yourself believe. If you believe then others will. Remember camouflage is also a kind of invisibility.'

I tried again. It didn't work. But, but, there was something in the way the guard coughed before he made his challenge, I was not imagining it, this kind of subtlety I could recognize, he coughed in a way respectful, as if he knew me, as if for a moment he thought me more important than I was. For a second, he believed I was Sir Miles, for a second.

I was excited but Dr Ragab, when I told him, said, 'These tricks are merely tricks. They attract the unworthy like meat attracting flies.'

'Could a thief learn how to be invisible?' I asked.

'It would only be possible if he were thieving for some better purpose, bread for someone starving for example, which is one reason such theft is not condemned in this country – unlike yours, I believe. But the important point is that greed disables all attempts to circumvent the fabric of ordinary experience. Greed is such a powerful emotion it is like a motorcar horn drowning out the sound of a cicada. And fear, being the same emotion as greed but its reverse, has the same effect. Only the thief who thieves for no reason save a love of thieving, if you like, and has no intention of profiting from his thieving, and has no fear of being caught, *no fear at all*, only he may learn to be invisible.'

'A thief without fear or greed is an unusual thief.'

Dr Ragab smiled a thin smile. 'The secret protects itself.'

But even here my mistake was in thinking that the dramatic was the important. All along it was the little things, the asides, the soft spoken throwaway lines that contained the real nutrition.

At long last. This is what I have been waiting for. Something simple. Strange – yes, inexplicable – maybe, but doable – I think so. The dot method of invisibility – for beginners. Even a doubting ignoramus such as myself should be able to follow the above instructions. All I needed was the right opportunity.

I had taken to following Cheryl around; well, not really following, more sort of driving past her house just to see if she was in, happened to be weeding in the front garden, that sort of thing. Not that often, I hasten to add. Just if I happened to be passing.

Bunkermania leads you this way. Security, secrecy, paranoia. You start imagining barriers that don't exist. You start to peep and pry. I knew all that. But I wasn't a stalker, a sicko, I was an observer, nothing more.

It was only when I was in the neighbourhood, waiting for invisibility opportunities.

Back to Hertwig.

39

In Dr Ragab's study stood a glass case. Behind leaded panes the shelves held rows of ceramic *shabtis*, *tebu* boomerangs, a worked flint scalpel, Roman funerary jewellery and a pre-dynastic diorite palate. On the lowest shelf was a box of a kind I recognized from the Cairo Museum: a papyrus-scroll library chest probably dating from the Ptolemaic period, thickly bound with bronze straps, made of palm wood black as ebony. Dr Ragab opened it for the first time the day I left.

'I want you to have these,' he said. From inside the chest he took two pieces of natural silica glass. 'No one knows how it's made. It is the purest natural glass in the world, found as you may know in the Great Sand Sea. The Pharaohs esteemed it and made their pectoral scarabs from it. Always keep a piece with you.'

Earlier that morning I had had a conversation with the Doctor, one of many I later forgot then remembered, on the next stage of invisibility. 'Oh, that,' he said, 'you just keep trying to see a candle through your hand – and do it in front of a mirror – it's easier. Six hundred attempts is a usual number before success. Then there is the special phrase *noor shekler redeed*, or is it *reddeed*? But really this kind of thing is just a distraction.'

'But it saved your life.'

'Look at it this way: if I had been more perceptive I wouldn't have needed the skill.'

Now I was leaving, I asked, 'Am I a good student?'

Dr Ragab looked thoughtful. 'No,' he replied, 'but you are my only student.'

I wanted to show him how keen I was to return. But the proof would always be in the returning, not in the 'sincere' tone of voice in which I said: 'I'll be back as soon as I can.' I need not have bothered, Dr Ragab had already turned away.

But before I could reach the ferry he had Suleiman run after me with a cabah, a yellow leather money bag with ten Maria Therese dollars inside, enough for the return journey from Europe.

40

In our family house my father lay in bed upstairs and stared for hours at a carriage clock with its back removed; the expansion and contraction of the movement calmed him, my mother said. Denied the clock he would scratch at the strange spreading bruise which the doctor said was unimportant.

Silent in the darkened upstairs room my father could only mouth words with great difficulty. 'Good,' he said. (Or was he saying 'God'? Surely not.) I read the word on his lips and imagined I heard it, but I did not. Every time I looked up I saw my father staring at me with eyes unlovely with terror, humourless, brazen with fear.

I was shocked that someone who had been so 'present' was mortal after all. And I was shocked by his craven cowardice, his utter fear in the face of death. I was shocked at the power of these old and new emotions even though I had transferred some sense of fatherhood by then to Dr Ragab.

The next morning my father was dead.

My first thought was: Who will look after me now? That made me ashamed. We cannot imagine the passing of time, we cannot imagine such absences. We think by analogy and then find ourselves ill with unexplained grief. Dr Ragab had armoured me against such a loss, but even armour leaves you bruised from the immensity of a direct blow. (I had thought that death would be an area of expertise and constant disquisition by Dr Ragab, but seldom if ever did he speak of it. As for revelations of what might happen on 'the other side', I was left with diminished apprehension but a sense of growing, though wordless, mystery. When I once pressed him for more information he said, 'I'll tell you one thing – if I survive this life without dying I'll be surprised.')

Driving around I discovered where Dick Bradawl's office was. A little way out of the City in a brand-new building parked between two old and venerable blocks like a giant shiny stainless-steel rubbish bin. Even the very edifice was odious. Was I the only one who could see that? Was the world blind? Was Cheryl blind? She must be because on one of my low passes past Bradawl Towers (actually No. 1 Eastgate) I saw her entering the building in a long skirt, fashionably unfashionable, carrying a black portfolio case as big as a French window.

Since I was in surveillance mode, i.e. I didn't want to be caught spying, I almost ducked down so she wouldn't see me. Instead I practised becoming a dot. I knew now you just had to visualize it. The rest was practice, and necessity. The first kind of invisibility was good enough for me – be perceived as insignificant, unseen in the way a dull advertisement in a newspaper is unseen.

Cheryl is the kind of person who is very observant though she has no interest in cars which is why she probably didn't see my car. But she didn't see me either.

OK. She was a long way away. But it was a start.

I called her that night just to check.

'Why haven't you been calling?'

'I have. I mean I am.'

'You are now. I meant before.'

'Been a bit busy. Research. That aluminium book.'

'Tell me a good aluminium fact, then.'

'Er. The Chinese invented aluminium three thousand six hundred years before we did. We know because an archaeological dig unearthed an aluminium comb that was buried in 1700 BC. The mystery is – you need electricity to make aluminium so did they discover that too?'

'The Chinese discovered everything.'

'They didn't discover the zero. That was the Arabs.'

'I thought it was the Indians.'

'One of the two. So what have you been up to?'

'Not much.'

She would have said if she'd seen me. She hadn't seen me because I'd been invisible.

There was a long pause.

'Guess what?' she asked.

'What?'

'I'm doing an installation in an office block. Lots of money.'

'A bank kind of office block? A Bradawl kind of bank.'

'Maybe.'

'It's a pay-off. A bribe.'

'We'll see.'

We'll see. I didn't like the sound of that at all.

When I returned to Hertwig's story I read on with a different level of concentration. I read on without the comfort of irony.

41

Twelve years sped by as if in a dream. (That can really happen, by the way, especially if you inhabit the future as we all did then.) After the variety and vigour of the East it seemed to me that Europe was half asleep, or hovering on the brink of a great slumber. In this I was to be proved entirely wrong, unless one can call the events that followed the sleepwalking of demented souls.

My only memories of that time are of brief isolated events, as if coming up for air from deep hibernation.

One thing I can never forget from that time was a vivid dream, or rather a nightmare, that came to me every few months for several years. It always began with the sound of voices, but these then became somehow terrible, speaking a language I had never heard before, a language I can only describe as being *without vowels*. No language on earth can exist without vowel sounds of some kind; therefore it was not of this earth. It is hard to imagine the complete terror I felt on hearing these voices speaking without vowels, it struck me as a pure malevolence.

Life punishes us not through circumstances but through our reaction to circumstances. We all receive warnings, one or two marvellous opportunities, angels looking out for us until they feel ignored. Suffice it to say my father's death made me panic.

I remained in Germany and was soon caught up in the hysteria of *becoming*. My knowledge of Arabic gained me a prestigious university position. I revived old friendships, including one with a woman I had known since childhood. Marriage, an uncontested divorce, a spate of poor health, and triumph over my colleagues took up seven years. Seven years of looking over my shoulder. My wife was clever, manipulative and ordinary; an intellectual and a supporter of the leader. 'Have you noticed the beauty of his hands?' she once remarked. 'Do you not grasp the connection between this and his stewardship of the land?' In seven years I was eminently successful in the small way of things. I became a senior university lecturer, teaching younger folk about the mysterious languages of the Orient.

All this time I was thinking of returning to Dr Ragab. I had forgotten my anger at the East, the imagined insults. Once I even booked a ticket but an 'important' occasion forced me to cancel. Real neglect of others follows no decision. It is another symptom of sleep. Dr Ragab, of course, knew this. I was surprised at how he kept me at a distance. And even at a distance he could be annoying. I sent him irregular gifts by mail and he would send a late perfunctory reply, rarely thanking me. Once he sent me a clipping from the London *Times*. It was an article about a German expedition to find the Pillars of Seth. Emil Kasparius, newly commissioned into Himmler's 'special collection' brigade, would lead it. But as I heard no more I assume he was unsuccessful.

Slowly, as I became enmeshed in the ways of the world, the need to get ahead, compete with my colleagues, make and spend money, give others their false due as they give you yours, over time that makes something like the Universal Language seem as obscure as that poetry you stayed awake memorizing in youth as if it mattered more than anything else. When did I last memorize a poem? Or even read one?

Gradually the political situation worsened. Even the university rector, a noted philosopher, appeared in a uniform of his own devising. He tried to encourage others to adopt his ludicrous 'authentic' thinker's garb. He wore breeches and calf-skin gaiters that buttoned to below the knee; boots were well nailed with triple hobs, a pattern favoured by farming folk; his shirts were light brown, all of them identical. He was always pleased to see students wearing similar clothing. And this man was supposed to teach philosophy! The love of wisdom!

By then I was living alone in the small university town, awake at last to the dire political situation, but unsure, fretting about what to do. It was then I decided to build the bunker. My father's great lake house had been empty for several years. None of the family wished to live there. The grounds were remote, deep in the forest. It would be the ideal place to escape the insanity that was engulfing Germany.

I had loved the lake since childhood. Several miles long, glass-clear water, a mirror set in the great forest, but all I could think about was the bunker, getting underground, becoming self-sufficient in a place where I could escape from our own marauding armies and those that I sensed surrounded our nation. Like the man in the parable with one talent, I sought to bury myself, my wealth, my potentiality.

42

It seems extraordinary to me that I, an academic, and not in the least bit practical, largely built that bunker myself and by hand. Krendl, the old family gardener, helped me with the concreting but I dug and built it myself (and used nails, unlike my father). Looking back now it is as if another person did it. And perhaps another did. The need for distraction from what I ought to do forced the growth of this new 'practical' personality, immersed in the details of concrete footings and joist supports. Because I had forgotten the word *gringul* I thought I had simply 'changed'. *Gringul* involves the movement from one self to another – in exaggerated form it manifests itself as multiple personalities – yet all of us to a greater or lesser extent have selves we wear like roles in a theatrical performance. *Gringul* uses the theatrical motif to explain the workings of the mechanism. This is the hard part, switching at will, from one role to another. In a play the director shouts 'old man' and you crouch into a similitude of ageing. In a blink you can jump up and 'play' a naughty infant in the classroom. What holds us back in 'real' life is how seriously we take the roles we play. As the mask becomes more cosy and familiar it gets harder to take off. Others prefer we wear only one mask. The world conspires with passports and *ausweis* to convince us we are unitary selves. *Gringul* is like an actor's exercise. Fasten on a key characteristic of the self you want to play, a look, a posture, a walk, a phrase, and use that to lead you into the role.

With excitement I laid out the foundations for the bunker in the green meadow. Krendl worked alongside me, a man who could be trusted, who refused to use the new greeting and always said 'Gruss Gott'. It was a sunny day and the grass sparkled with dew. The little aluminium boat my grandfather had used lay across the line of my proposed footings, face down fringed by longer grass.

I hooked my boot under the gunwale of the boat and lifted it up high enough to get a grip with my hands. It was a hot day and I was surprised to see two vipers coiled together on top of the ropes in the dank pale grass. Their bodies were so entwined that I did not see them as two snakes, at first I thought it just one long snake, glabrous and diamond-backed in the released heat of the lifted boat. The snakes slid over each other, black cog markings against orange and grey, the coils pumping free with slick ease. One headed north, one south, wavering between grass stems like something sliding out from between a strong grip.

The viper has no strength during its hibernation and no poison in its fangs. By April they are ready to bite. Then it was July and such snakes were best avoided. Old Krendl cheered when he saw the vipers. 'Them'll be a house snake for you! That's good luck, that is.'

Unfortunately I had to halt my reading at this point as I had mislaid the manuscript, which was very, very unusual for me. I am careful about my things, I never lose notebooks and have maybe lost only one or two books in my entire life. I searched the flat high and low. I began to suspect it had been stolen. Perhaps by a burglar who left no traces and expertly jemmied the 'drug-dealer' and then relocked it . . .

When Cheryl rang to invite me to the private view of her installation at Bradawl Towers I politely declined. She was surprised and that pleased me and then I realized I would have to deny myself the pleasure of actually going.

As I searched for the manuscript in all the places I had already looked I made some new resolutions. Out of a sense of self-preservation I should cut myself off from Cheryl. In her place I should turn in greater earnest to my hobbies. Except I don't really have any. Drinking alone is not a hobby. Reading *After the Battle* magazine is not a hobby. Talking about bunkers is not a hobby. These are distractions, not hobbies. Hobbies involve implementing something. Action.

Action. I left the flat to pace the streets of Ealing. I bought a coffee at the 7-Eleven and stared in the window of a travel agent as I sipped it. Flights abroad were really cheap! I saw that Egypt was a popular destination and it set me thinking. I had recently discovered in *After the Battle* magazine there was a huge Italian bunker complex yet to be really explored a short distance from the battlefields of El Alamein. In the same article mention was made of the secret Caves at Mersa Matruh, from whence Rommel commanded his troops plus a map reference for several old Carro Veloce CV33 tankettes half buried in the sand. I had never really been drawn to the ruins and remains of ancient Egypt, they seemed too well documented, sucked dry by tourists and archaeologists. Not enough metal. But these modern remains drew my avid attention.

As soon as I decided, half decided, almost decided to visit Egypt I found the manuscript again. But not where I left it. I am sure of that . . . almost sure.

43

In 1937 Hagar arrived out of the blue. I took it as a sign although I knew such thinking was probably foolish. She had graduated from the American University in Beirut; subsequently she applied to our faculty to study the origin of certain 'Western' tales in the *Thousand and One Nights*. I was attached to the folklore department but she was not my student. Her parents had long ago divorced, her father finding his German film career prospered after he re-married an Aryan actress. He was not very welcome in Egypt by then, except by the likes of Prince Tamar, the notorious pro-Nazi. Hagar's mother lived in Berlin where she drank Tokay and bitters for breakfast and consorted with leftists and bohemians. She received an invitation from Bertrand Viertel, as did many Jewish artists, to work in Hollywood. There, whilst driving alone along a canyon at night, her Studebaker left the road and overturned. She might have survived but the accident happened on a holi-day weekend. No one noticed her disappearance. When a lone policeman finally investigated the wreck he found her famous features already dissolving in the California sun.

Hagar still had her short silvery blonde curly hair, her sharp-edged, well-defined mouth, her boyish frame. The leg had never properly mended and she wore a caliper that made her limp. She never remarked on it and never complained. Though once, and this was when she was in the bunker, apropos of nothing she said, 'This is God's punishment of my father and mother, not me – it upset them more than me to see me imperfect.'

Hagar had a German passport. Halfway through her studies I urged her to leave, to fly to America or even Uruguay. She would not. Then it was stamped with a large medieval 'J' and she could not leave the country. It was too late. She was stuck.

I have mentioned the 'swap' system at the university. Jewish students, now officially disallowed on PhD programs, could be assigned informally to a teacher other than the one they officially were registered with. This allowed us to keep teaching.

I saw Hagar most days, and yet still I did not seek to encourage anything more than the normal relations between teacher and student. Out of innate respect and bedazzlement at her luminous soul I could not, unlike our dear rector, who philandered eagerly with students keen for his attention, allow myself to show my true feelings for her. Besides they seemed a little ridiculous even to myself. Perhaps that was the real reason. I was not Dante, and these were not Dante's times. On the conscious level, one meeting, nine years earlier, was insufficient to explain how often I thought of her in the intervening years. Now she was here I understood she was what Dr Ragab meant when he spoke of luminous souls. Frequently they are born under difficult conditions, often abandoned, a good proportion die young and great numbers of ordinary people attend their funerals and yet don't quite know why. Luminous souls do not smile all the time, but when they do, that smile is utterly contagious. It circles the planet faster than Ariel with outspread wings. If luminous souls whistle or sing, there is a lightening of everyone's mood, all burdens cease to be felt. Put a luminous soul at the head of an army and you will see victory after victory, but they will only rarely accept such a task. Luminous souls are never artists except during special times. In fact they appear as resolutely normal, not superior in any way except for this intangible luminosity that lights their way, lightens our lives. The funny thing is, most people can't see it and even ignore these people who could so benefit them.

Then the 'swap' system came under suspicion.

She did not look 'Jewish' according to the caricature advice printed in newspapers that my estranged wife loved to read. But she was well known, as the offspring of actors. It did not help that her father had disowned her.

The rector asked that we complete a list of Jewish students recently taught, such lists would soon be used to hunt down and imprison the innocent.

It was then that the idea came to me that Hagar could hide at the lake house – better, she could hide in the bunker, a bunker that no one, apart from the reliable old Krendl, knew about.

It had the makings of a perfect solution so Hagar of course said no. The situation deteriorated. Owing to my previous war service and injuries I was never going to be conscripted. But I saw little point in continuing my teaching. I resigned, and this persuaded Hagar I was genuine in my offer. Telling no one, we left for the forest together.

Years passed. War crossed and re-crossed the land. Deep in the forest we knew little of this. On very rare occasions we were visited and Hagar would hide. Nothing of hers was ever left outside the bunker – and she always slept there, strange though that may seem.

We worked hard, living by the seasons, hunting and gathering food from the woods, enjoying the sunlight that came down slanting through the trees. But it was the idyll of a dream not reality. At night we heard aeroplane engines overhead, and later we saw the American daytime bomber raids, hordes of great silver birds high in the sky heading for Berlin and Leipzig.

Once a plane crashed on the far side of the lake. We saw its fiery tail (at night the planes belched fire from their exhausts) expand into a comet arcing to the ground. At dawn the home guard from ten miles away drove in on hay carts. They found one forlorn New Zealand boy, the only survivor, and took him away to a Luftwaffe prison camp.

We lived like people from another gentler age while all around us the war carried on its business. Our mistake was to think we had escaped once the fighting had ceased.

44

I woke up that day at the lake house with a strange presentiment of joy. Everything was alive. The woods and the lake were perfect in themselves. I saw that for years I had been comparing them to an image I had of perfection, rather than just looking and seeing what they were.

I heard a bird sing for the first time since, when? For years, almost, it seemed, since I was in the desert with Ragab and watched a crested hoopoe open its beak with a 'huk-huk' sound, its silhouette sharp against the rock in the heat, and saker falcons gliding in high circles, calling high-pitched and far away an almost human cry.

Hagar was in a foul mood, which brought me down to earth. When a luminous soul is in a bad mood the effect is usually humorous.

That day, Hagar gathered wild celandines, bluebells and cornflowers and stood them in a vase on the kitchen table. I looked intently at them, seeing some new significance in their colour and shape.

'Be careful with those flowers, please!' said Hagar. 'They took a long time to arrange.'

Something was happening. Something had happened. I was sure of it.

'Look, you've messed them up!'

'I was only looking,' I said, amused. For some reason I thought: now is the time to leave for Egypt.

At the same moment Hagar said, 'I was just thinking, that it was about time we left this depressing place. We should visit Egypt.'

How would you explain that? Telepathy?

Once, a few winters ago, I was out on the frozen lake. Wind had scoured away most of the snow, leaving ripples in the surface. Even at the edge there was no creaking or movement as I stepped off the land. I set out walking to the island, which was a good two kilometres away. On and on I went, not sliding on the ice but walking carefully. We had a dog then, in the first year of the war, and its claws clattered against the surface.

The first crack-boom I thought was a gun shot in another valley. Then I saw the crack lines spread like something being thrown. The cracks pinged and shuddered the surface as if they were not solid but made of rubber.

Hagar was already at the lakeside. Then she waded back up her snow tracks to the house. Twenty yards from the shore I saw her at the top of the slope with the long ladder we used for pruning the highest tree branches. I waved, began to shout, 'I'm all right now,' when the ice collapsed and I fell into freezing water. The dog yelped and scrabbled with leaden claws at loose upended blocks of ice. Then he got to solid ice and Hagar pulled him out by the collar. I broke off chunks of ice to reach the ladder's end and with great effort dragged myself onto the rungs. I lay exhausted, feeling my coat freeze to my body in the chill air.

She was supposed to have gone to the village that

afternoon. Why did she stay? How did she know? Telepathy. She told me she just hadn't felt like cycling in the cold.

Hagar was right – why not leave now? The packing would not be difficult: two cardboard suitcases filled with old clothes. The important thing: valid passports and visas I understood we could get at the new administrative centre.

The only transport we had were our two rusty bicycles, but they were enough to get us to the railway station. Hagar packed while I got them ready. One had a puncture.

Hagar groaned when she saw me at work. 'You're going to take ages, I can tell.'

I had the important thing hoarded – rubber cement. I waved it triumphantly.

Hagar looked past me. 'I think I saw someone coming along the lake edge.'

I could see nothing but the sun's reflection off the water and the greenness of beech trees in early leaf. 'Probably just a poacher.'

'If you'd mended that tyre earlier we wouldn't have to find out.'

We had had visitors before. Deserting soldiers, both German and American – we always gave them food. 'They'll only take it otherwise,' said Hagar.

I finished the repair and held the bicycle experimentally by the handlebars and seat, bouncing the tyre on the gravel.

'All right, well done, now can we please go?' said Hagar, sitting astride the other bike with her suitcase tied to the rack.

'Just a minute, I think your chain could do with some oil.'

Hagar rolled her eyes upwards.

I went round to the lean-to generator shed where I kept such precious supplies. When I got back Hagar had tied my suitcase onto my rack for me.

'What's the hurry?'

She sighed.

'I'll just lock up, then.'

But after pocketing the big key for the front door I wanted to linger.

'Do you think it's worth nailing the ground-floor shutters closed?'

'No.' She gave me a look – a look that in future I would always pay attention to.

'I think I'll just nail them shut.'

I couldn't find enough nails in the generator shed so I had to unlock the back door to get some from inside. When I came out Hagar pointed in the lake's direction at three figures loping along the shore. 'We should go *now*.'

'They're only children!'

As they came closer I saw they were not children. They waved in a friendly way.

'*Now!*' Hagar turned her own bike as if to start riding.

'Two minutes. They're probably starving.' I had a strong feeling I was resisting Hagar out of pure habit.

The one in front, the thinnest, his thinness exaggerated by a tall rabbit-fur hat, was smiling. He had long fingers and though patched, his clothes had an indefinable neatness about them. Not so the second, who wore odd socks like a clown, red and green. He had a clown's carrot hair and dirty prominent teeth. The last was dark from the sun, also thin, in a worn blue boiler suit, the same colour as his eyes.

Around their waists hung squirrels, songbirds and rabbits looped through their own pelts. Over their shoulders were rolled US Army blankets and well-made bows. Each man had a cloth quiver of arrows tipped with crow's feathers at his waist. It gave them a quaint look but we were used to it, many farmers hunted with bows after the Americans collected the Reich's weapons.

'What do you want? Food? Cabbage? Carrots? Bread? We have bread.'

The one in odd socks whistled without taking his eyes off me. A great lively shepherd dog broke through the rhododendron bushes. Bounding straight for me it seized me by the ankle in a ridiculous posture that caused me to fall over.

Hagar did not intervene. And being a luminous soul they did not know what to do with her.

They knew about the bunker, however – how I don't know. I could tell by the way one went and lifted the logs that hid the outside entrance. Krendl? But Krendl was dead, killed by the starvation of the previous winter. Regardless of how they knew, they looked as if they already had a plan, something worked out. They forced me underground and locked the door.

45

Having come full circle I remember even in the bunker the habit of procrastination remained. I put off my escape attempt with endless practice.

Wow, faal, szaz, shem.

Practising made me hungry and I noticed, not for the first time, that the food was getting better. I was sure Hagar was cooking for the thugs. For one thing, the vegetables came in a kind of pattern on the soup. Only Hagar would do something like that.

Wow, faal, szaz, shem.

What did Dr Ragab say? There is never a perfect time for anything, only a right time. It was time for *noor shakler redeed*, or was it *noor shakkler redeed*? I was not certain if the extra emphasis made a difference. The Doctor had mentioned the words only once, throwing the lines away as if they were not important.

Before I delivered the correct phrase I needed to start from where I left off.

I imagined myself disappearing to a point, a dot. You must see yourself as a transparent skeleton, then that shrinks, too, to point zero.

The dot still causes the viewer to see an image, even something they recognize, though crucially they do not react to it. This cannot work for very long however. It's important to also remember that one remains invisible only so far as no other sense is engaged. Using the dot method, if you are touched by someone the illusion is exposed.

The next step is to reduce oneself to the dot and then enlarge as someone, or thing, that will cause no response, or a frightened response. Instead of seeing an escaped prisoner they see their leader Mr Particular. I must *become* Mr Particular (or Oddsocks or Roy or even Hagar – but it is better if the person they see is one they wish to avoid) in the way an actor *becomes* the part he plays. There is nothing magical in it but it does require conviction. This method works well – but only if one person is looking at you. If your conviction falters, multiple observers can cause it to fail.

Total invisibility to all requires adroit movement through the earlier stages, which are merely the precursor, or basic condition, of the real skill, which is projection of the appropriate phrase in the Universal Language through every fibre of one's being. The projection is the hard part.

I observed my mind thinking how futile the whole thing was; I imagined myself giving up. But I didn't give up.

I remembered what Ragab said, this was mechanical, almost anyone could do it, a mere side effect of the real understanding of the Universal Language. Nothing to it. I needed only to do as he advised so long ago, placing a candle behind my hand and then looking at its reflection in the mirror.

I lacked only a candle. I could use the mirror as my

light source but then I would have no mirror to check the reflection. There was nothing for it but to break the mirror in two – use one to reflect the light from the shaft and one to check the progress of my invisibility.

I scored with the nail a line back and forth deep into the silvering of the mirror. Then with shirt wrapped hands I heaved on the glass.

It shattered into a thousand useless pieces. None of them large enough to reflect the light.

46

I prayed in earnest now. But it was wrong. All real prayer, I suspect, is giving thanks and I was not. I knelt with my forehead on the floor. There was no point even in suicide, which struck me as an almost humorous option. The depths of self-pity take one past suicide and into a place of pure helplessness. Suicide requires one to actually want to do something. Apathy undermines even the desire to destroy oneself.

For no reason I could articulate I reached towards the food tray which I knew to be in front of me. I could see nothing because I had taken the food into the main bunker room, which could not be illuminated now the mirror was broken. On the soup's surface: two pods, always two – which struck me fancifully as representing the pillars supporting the roof of the bunker. Between the pods a sprout. The daily sprout. Pay attention, that meant. Beneath the sprout was a line of three peas. The drain pipes that had stored the wine were arranged in blocks of three. It was a map.

I had felt inside each pipe a hundred times. It was not that. The gap between each drainpipe was packed with cement separating it from the row above. The pipe ends stuck out hiding the join.

I got closer, pulling and grabbing at the pipes. I tried to pull each pipe out but they extended a mere centimetre or so from flush – not enough grip. Then I understood. I pushed my arms deep into two pipes and locked them there with a clenched fist. I pulled back and with a grinding sound the middle three-by-three section of pipes came away.

It revealed a cleverly cut square hole, quite shallow. In it was a salt shaker, silver; a box of matches and a tin box; in the box a spirit lamp and a blue bottle of methylated spirit. There was also a sketchbook full of Hagar's watercolours and a piece of silica glass I gave her, one of the two I was given by Dr Ragab.

Hagar had not forgotten me.

47

I started to practise. The aim was to see the spirit lamp flame through the obstruction of my hand. I watched for the flame in a splinter of glass left over from the broken mirror – it was enough. You transfer all your attention to the hidden light and when you see it the hand is, for that moment, invisible. I started intoning: *noor shakkler redeed*, that was the right pronunciation I was sure. Once, twice, three times . . . three hundred times, three hundred and one. Each attempt took about thirty seconds. Each attempt drained me of, for want of a better word, psychic energy.

Six hundred and eight, six hundred and nine. I could barely keep my eyes open. Six hundred should suffice, Ragab had said.

I was up to a thousand. A thousand and one. Not a glimmer. I kept going until I was seeing double from all the strain. I rubbed my eyes and tried again. Still two hands reflected in the mirror shard. But only one lamp flame! Without the mirror, and slowly fading now, I saw two hands, two arms. Instead of disappearing I had made myself quite literally twice as visible.

48

The phrase was wrong. I realized that immediately. Had this been intended by Dr Ragab? Surely not consciously? Yet something had worked. This gave me immense hope. I had not, I think, really believed before. Now I did. Everything was getting clearer now. My energies were reviving.

I started again, this time intoning the sentence without the second hard 'k'. After six hundred more tries I saw the first faint flickering of a blue flame, a ghostly image through my hand. I concentrated and it disappeared. I looked at the edge of the image, looked around it not at it. Three hundred tries later and I could see through my hand. I had made it invisible, for about two or three seconds.

The next step was to increase the amount of body I could make disappear. I wound out the wick of the tiny lamp to make it brighter. Then I stood with the light behind me and imagined that I could see it through my leg. That took about two hundred repeated attempts.

49

My periods of comparative transparency grew. I timed myself by counting off the seconds: one thousand and one, one thousand and two, one thousand and three – counting always helped to keep my mind clear of fear and greed: to remain invisible I needed to maintain the mental state of not *wanting* to be invisible. Each day I made my image less distinct, more ghostly, till at last: nothing. Then I extended the periods of perfect invisibility. At around half a minute I reached what seemed to be my limit. I was ready. *Noor shakler redeed.*

I crouched in the dark, pressed against the wall under the shaft, waiting. The click of the padlock signalled the start. I forced myself to see the dot in front of my mind's eye. Slowly I felt myself physically shrinking, smaller and smaller. The sound of the bolt. I repeated *noor shakler redeed*, measuring my breathing against each letter pronounced. And slowly I began to see the wall through my arm. Some odd vibration in what I saw but increasingly transparent.

I was taken by surprise when the trap opened. They let down the fish kettle for the dirty plates. I did not move.

They grew impatient and jangled the fish kettle against the floor. There was a muttering and someone must have fetched a torch because a powerful light shone in. I looked away. I was invisible, I knew it.

'Where is he?'

'Asleep.'

'Where?'

They shouted and banged very loudly then hauled up the kettle. The trapdoor slammed shut. Then it was bolted.

Minutes went by. I became visible again and climbed a short way up the shaft – I did not want to bump into them when they came to investigate. It all depended on being ready. I could not remain invisible except in bursts. I prepared myself for the next encounter. No greed, no fear. Use greed to destroy fear – what had the upper hand – greed for escape – so I concentrated hard on all the things that might happen to me when they caught me. Fear began to dominate. I thought of Hagar, but very briefly. *Noor shakler redeed.*

The sound of the bolt again. I was invisible almost immediately. Then the trapdoor lifted. More banging of pots. The light swept through me to the foot of the shaft. The trapdoor shut. Only seconds later came the sound of the key in the bunker's outer door. Careful footsteps, two men, Oddsocks and Roy – Mr Particular would be elsewhere, watching. The key in the inner door. Don't think about Hagar. Of course I do. Focus on counting. One thousand and one.

The bunker door banged open. Oddsocks entered with a torch. Roy, I think it was Roy, waited in the doorway up the short flight of steps. One thousand and two. Oddsocks looked up the shaft, looked through me and then looked around the bunker. One thousand and three.

'He isn't here.'

Roy jumped down three steps at once and turned to look in the privy. One thousand and four.

My chance and I took it. I had bare feet, better that way, soundlessly I dropped from the shaft. Oddsocks' torch swept the interior. Its light shone through my head. They knew something was wrong.

'Check under that fucking bed.'

I was through the door and running.

Almost into Mr Particular. He stood blocking the stairs. Beyond him, outlining his form, was the early evening gloom which seemed like broad daylight to me. His eyes were deep set, not dead eyes, far from it, but unblinking eyes, blue, dark greyish tinged blue with a fleck pattern of black and irises that reflected . . . not me, I looked down and away and he looked through me. What was I up to? A thousand and ten. A thousand and eleven – I could not get past.

I could hear his breathing and listened for an age. Did I dare to knock him down? Only half a thought, speculative, unsure, fearful. A thousand and twenty.

He shouted right into me, 'What's going on? What's happening down there?'

Footsteps rushed, as if following orders, coming from behind. He moved down a step and I lifted each leg with care over his. One thousand and thirty. Now I was moving up the stair past him. Then, at the last moment, he looked my way and I saw my own form shudder into visibility. I lost concentration. Just his look had unnerved me.

'Here!'

I barged through the outside door into the starlit night. The sudden experience of being outdoors caused my spirit to rise, to float free despite the fear. Then I was running barefoot for the darkened woods.

I bent low through the pines. Water sprayed from disturbed boughs. My bare feet I didn't even think about. I could see the moon running through the branches above. I must be near the main track soon I thought, and I was. Now I was quite visible. Up one side of the track, visible on the skyline and down the other. Into the ditch my feet splashed in the stream as I stumbled towards something only I knew about: a culvert, less than a metre across, hidden by bushes. *Well hidden.* I broke through the bushes and plunged into the metre-high drain that went under the track. I crawled to the far end, also hidden by bushes. My chest shuddered to get enough air. After a long while I risked looking out. Nothing. I must have lost them in the woods.

I turned to feel hot breath on my shoulder. It was the shepherd dog, grinning, with its pink juicy tongue and sharp teeth ready to bite.

50

In the lake house, on the long table in the great hall, they secured me at the feet and hands using fencing wire.

I turned my face and saw the piano with its back stove in. They had taken care to break everything except the mirrors for some reason. The broken windows allowed a damp breeze from the forest to blow through the place.

I twisted my head to look about me. Mr Particular leant towards me and slapped my face hard. It was extraordinarily humiliating.

Mr Particular had a passion for collecting things and arranging them. At the head of the table was a tray with a row of old screws and nails in descending order of size.

He spent a while looking at his collection. His light breathing was apparent as he selected a large masonry nail. He hefted a rusty claw hammer in the other hand, weighing it. Roy brought down all his weight on my wrist, flattening it against the table. With his delicate sense of control Mr Particular prodded the nail point into the palm of my hand. I involuntarily flexed it shut.

Irritated at my presumption he unfurled my fist and jammed the point under my middle fingernail as if he wanted to clear the circle of dirt from underneath. Then he hammered it home, driving deep into the soft under-flesh of the finger. He then extracted it, wrenching the fingernail out at an angle. Sick agony clouded my head. I must have passed out, though it seemed as if I retained a vague consciousness. I sensed terrible dreams around me. They dragged me out face down the bunker stairs and threw me back into my prison hole.

I put the story down for a moment on the edge of the basin – just for a moment – I was in the bathroom – reading whilst shaving – trying to finish it before going out in the evening – when the manuscript fell into the soapy water. Disaster. Fool. Usually I am never this clumsy. I'm falling apart. Or something. I fished it out and spread the pages all over the greyish white carpet of the living room. I dropped over each page a piece of kitchen roll, peering anxiously under each sheet to see if the ink had run – it had. So I had to rush from page to page blotting madly and carefully.

I turned on the heater and shut all the windows. By the time I returned I hoped it would be dry.

My reason for going out: a pathetic desire to see Cheryl – on neutral ground (that night it was Freddy Boleras' exhibition at the Coalhole) rather than at her own exhibition or installation or whatever it was.

I got there quite early and after a quick patrol of the smoky gallery I saw no one I knew. I drank wine and looked at Freddy's pictures which were on plywood laid on the floor. They featured gouged and painted numerals, as if Jasper Johns had gone mad with a chisel. The chiselled grooves were filled with white powder, perhaps an ironic nod at Freddy's Colombian nationality. Only one person seemed to be paying them much attention. Bradawl. Alone. No Cheryl in sight. I was fixated by the sight of him.

Hidden by others I examined his unremarkable face, his full lips, his ruddy complexion, a complexion I've noticed even Americans living temporarily in Britain can acquire, so it must be due to the weather or the food. Some Americans that is, usually wealthy ones. A horrible sort of envy crept over me that was unassuaged by knowing he had a metal bar through his prick. Then I broadened my view and saw that Bradawl was self-consciously alone and though in a flash suit with Berlutti shoes he knew, and everyone else knew, his demeanour was not that of an artist, bohemian or anyone in the art trade. Money often makes you at home but not always. Strangely I even felt sorry for Bradawl with his big lumbering frame (no doubt beaten into shape on the rugby fields of some of the finest public schools in England); his feeble attempt at buying cool by getting his bell end broached; his conformist lack of originality. And he looked so unlike his usual commanding self; sheepish, even, and that seemed wrong. I decided to say hello. Be nice to him. Just as I approached on my mercy mission Freddy hove into view already merry, his face red beneath the indigenous tribesman's 'nutcut' he's taken to sporting. I nodded at Freddy as I extended my hand with enthusiasm towards Bradawl.

The next bit happened in slow motion. At the moment of my approach Bradawl signalled pathetic eagerness at being noticed but in a split second he understood he had within his social orbit not just me but also the main man of the party, the focal point, albeit a short and pixelated focal point.

He hesitated, just enough to send a message. And then it came: 'I don't believe we've met?' Accompanied by a triumphal glint to the eye.

The English thing. Instead of saying, 'Of course we bloody well have,' I mumbled my name as if complying with an immigration official's enquiry. This all passed Freddy by who all the time continued nudging and whooping in Bradawl's face with some convoluted tale of Brit art farce and fame (Gavin Turk used to size Freddy's canvases). Freddy made the exaggerated inhalation sign of someone toking too long on a joint as the punchline and Bradawl laughed uproariously, in the manner of someone eager to show they are well into hashish themselves. In fact he was opening like a flower. It was as if the attention of others was like the sun, bronzing his skin in the very time we stood there. It all made sense. He was now best pals with the host and didn't need me. I was expendable, social cannon-fodder.

Snobbery isn't a crime. You have to accept it in England. You have to grow a thick skin. Knowing all this it can still take you by surprise, like a dead leg or a sudden punch to the solar plexus. I reeled away, my social bonhomie in ruins. For several minutes I hid by the grid of spotless wine glasses and then moved along to the food table, a tableclothed trestle loaded with fine cheeses, slivers of French bread, grapes, apples, bananas, and an enormous bowl of strawberries. One fine cheese, or not so fine, I didn't know, was a spherical Edam type cheese except the waxy outer layer was black instead of red. In my consternation at being snubbed I started absentmindedly kneading a lump of this black wax into a ball. That's when the idea came to me. Using a thick shiny knife I carved the wax ball into a shape the size of a sugar cube. Then I rounded the edges off. In a final flourish I smeared it with a small greasy sausage on a stick – it even smelt authentic.

People who like dope, but live regular lives, always find getting the stuff awkward. They don't want to have a supplier because that would seem like addiction. On the other hand, they like the odd smoke.

I walked up to Bradawl and said in a most friendly fashion, 'Here – I'm leaving – you have it, I don't need it – not now.'

His closed face relaxed with pleasurable anticipation. He even raised his eyebrow conspiratorially at the Silk Cut he held unlit. 'Hey, thanks, man,' and he patted me friendlily on the shoulder. Music. I had guessed Bradawl's position exactly. With loving care he pocketed the dud cube in his sharp suit pocket.

Later, when I got home, I imagined his disappointment but I didn't have anyone to share it with so it kind of fell flat. Then I had a horrible image, hard to lose, of Cheryl and him trying to smoke it together and finding it really funny.

Even though I don't usually read after having drunk several glasses of wine I started reading (the now dry) Hertwig again, it took my mind off that image.

51

You can put off ending only so long. My elaborate preparations, my absolute confidence, all for nothing. The intense pain of my injuries. I thought I had always been a doubter but fear meant I never acknowledged it. Some new pain occurred – a sudden flood of it in my chest. The pain wouldn't go. Maybe my heart – even in the depths of doubt I adopted the *szaz* position on the floor, kneeling, backside in the air, the way morphine addicts die. Slowly, imperceptibly, the pain lessened. The past was lies and wish-fulfilment. Religion a false shell of no utility. My finger hurt again – a good sign since it meant the chest pain couldn't have been serious. I, at last, way past the midpoint of my life, after the death of both parents, when even the most adolescent have managed to grow up, at last admitted I had fooled myself.

What a confluence of lies. *Noor shekler redeed.* With the strength that comes from loss of illusions I looked at my wrecked finger.

It wasn't there.

The pain. The shortcut I had ignored. It was effortless. No wavering of images, just the simple words enough. I remained thus for half an hour. All along I had been playing with my ideas of being 'in the present'. These criminals, these blundering idiots with their terrible lives, had taught me my final lesson, the one I needed.

But the pain did not last. I needed more of it I knew. Pain that I could control. The nail, the one I found in the winepipe, would serve me well.

The ceiling trusses were pegged to the joists and the pillars. Using the nail and my shoe I was able to knock the pegs out. This was not easy but when it was done I used the shoe to batter the heavy piece of oak out of its double tenons. Holding it like a brick the plank was a heavy usable hammer.

Around my injured finger I tightened a strip of cloth torn from my shirt. I twisted it and used my spoon as a tourniquet lever. The finger throbbed and throbbed and then became numb. I flicked it and it felt like flicking someone else's body.

My object was to drive the nail into the existing wound in my finger. I made a support out of wine-label paper to hold the nail in place.

I learnt one thing in the war. When you need to do something alone (with others it's easier) that will result in injury, it's best to be muddleheaded. Too much clear thinking sets your survival mechanism to work and you think up good reasons to back out. You need to become a little frenzied, crazy, your mind in turmoil. It was not difficult.

I raised my oak club, nothing less than full force. I hoped I would not hit bone. If I did . . . well, I hoped that I would not.

No.

Three times I drew back my makeshift hammer. There

was no other way. The frenzy at last held with no interrupting thought.

I hammered down as hard as I could. The exact memory now gone. Hammered down *hard*. Sudden moat of blood, eruption of anguish, a red bubble shiny red, a big bubble, a big red bubble. The nail went into the old scab, missed the bone and into the wooden floor pinning skin pinning my hand. I had my pain. My hand was on fire. There was no end to it but I waited for the wave of pain to settle, here was the key – the nail sticking right through could be twisted, pushed or knocked at any time to send a horrible reminder throughout my body forcing an instant clearance of irrelevance from the mind. Now fear had nowhere to hide, now greed could not take up residence.

The nail stuck through the glutinous mess in my finger with a rime of clear fluid around its point of entry and departure. The old fingernail I pulled off with interest and no especial increase in the pain. I examined my hand by the low wavering light from the mirror.

An hour or so later I worked the nail to produce workable pain, a deep, worrying, serious pain, yet a pain that was not fatal, except through some kind of infection or blood poisoning. I had a strong belief that I would not get ill. This was important, since pain always means something, and what it means decides, often, whether the pain is bearable or not. The strongest urge when we experience pain is to try and make it go away. I wanted to reverse this. For me it was imperative to prolong the agony, maintain the discomfort – this I knew would cause that surge of concentration I needed.

The banging was distant at first and I could not understand its source. Then there was cursing and a rending sound. Then hammering on the other side of the inner door. They were nailing up the entrance.

The only exit was the narrow chimney to the trapdoor, which they did not nail shut, yet. This was the endgame and no amount of optimistic interpretation could change the instant gloom created by such evidence. I was entombed, buried alive for sure now, only a matter of time.

52

They lowered a last meal. I knew it to be the last because when the rope was raised there was no sound of the bolt and padlock being secured above. They were already thinking of other things.

Another soup map, this time quite different. A concoction of a potato slice, two beans and twelve peas. I prodded them with all the seriousness of a haruspicator of ancient times. Were the peas indicative of sections of wall? No, it was clearly a clock. The time shown was 2 a.m. Then, as if driven by my thoughts, the trapdoor opened again. Something on a line descending, on a butcher's hook, it shook off with a clatter. I knew what it was. Hagar's leg iron. Aluminium with steel calipers.

I screamed with an anguish absorbed by the heavy wooden surrounds all too easily.

Then it began. I turned the nail deliberately. A slow unravelling at the edges of my vision, a lightening at the margins, as if lifting some raiment, letting in light. I felt the fullness of light inside me. I could see through the ceiling of my prison to the night sky above. I could see the trees moving. I had succeeded – not in making myself invisible – but my prison – in that glimpse I understood all the talk of ages, the talk of oneness, *yet knew it for just the beginning, the mere starting point* and then it went. But something remained. The eye and the eyes, the sun and the eyes. I am the observer and the observed.

Time passed almost instantly. I dipped my finger in the water-clock container, the time was 2 a.m., I drained the contents.

I climbed the chimney, slow, all breath measured, caved in on myself, slow with inadvertent pain, the nail proud of my finger. In one pocket I had the salt shaker in the other Dr Ragab's silica glass. Tied by a torn cloth strip to my ankle was Hagar's leg iron. I moved and it swung behind me in the narrow hole. Slowly, shuffling my back against the planks, I moved upwards. At the top I felt with my chin the top button of my shirt. I felt the button shape with great clarity.

My head could not get a grip on the lid underside, it slid out, the lid too heavy.

I gave up. Rested. I knew I was getting weaker. With all my neck muscles straining I got the lid to move a fraction – it was unlocked – but there was still weight on it. I shuffled higher and freed my good hand. With more purchase I got the lid a fraction open and saw the lighter darkness of the house.

The white tip of the dog's tail showed and with a clattering of claws the lid was suddenly light. I lifted it higher and smelt the dog's breath. I twisted the nail. *Noor shakler redeed.*

The dog could not see me but he smelt me. Through the crack of the lifted lid I saw the extended legs of Roy asleep in an armchair not a metre away.

With sweating slow difficulty I tipped salt into my palm, spat on it and made several large damp pellets. These I flung and the dog went after them, licking the floor. I hauled up Hagar's caliper, stuck it in my belt, then lifted the lid and climbed free.

Mr Particular came through the library doors with an olive-green gasoline can in his hand. He looked at the dog and then at the open shaft. He halted next to me. I could see the light stubble on his thin face, I could hear his breathing.

Roy awoke and stretched. Oddsocks came clanking through with two more twenty-litre cans. I did not move.

The dog, licking and whining at the floor, puzzled them all. Roy kicked its backside with vigour and its teeth showed white.

Mr Particular said, 'Who opened it?'

Roy shrugged.

Oddsocks emptied an entire glugging can of gasoline down the shaft. Mr Particular shone his torch down.

'Wait. Let's do this properly.'

He took an ACP pistol out of his pocket, a single-shot .45, dropped in vast numbers by the Americans to resistance groups, available in most DP camps. He fetched the rope ladder, unfurled it and climbed down, pistol in hand.

I touched the nail, and in my own veil of pain, took two steps and kicked over the open can resting at the edge of the shaft. Oddsocks fumbled for it and I pushed him. He saved himself but dropped the can down the shaft. From my pocket I tore four matches, struck and lit.

The shaft entrance exploded, a three-metre roaring

yellow flame. Dripping fire was upon Oddsocks' hands and Roy's hair. They beat madly at it. Then stopped. What held all our gaze, including the dog, was the emerging figure of Mr Particular, his head and shoulders a burning mass of flame, a human candle gripping the ladder he emerged from the shaft like a mechanical doll all afire and in his acute agony saw me, how I don't know, his eyes locked onto mine and he raised an arm to point but then the ropes burnt through and he fell down into the flaming vent.

Spilled gasoline spread fire across the floor and into the long curtains either side of the library door. All at once I caught the smell of gasoline in the roof of my mouth. I saw the empty cans lying with their levered lids unsecured on the stairs – the place had already been soaked in fuel, ready to burn down.

Heavy oak banisters, balustrades and the stair carpet burst into sudden blue-yellow flame of instant heat. I ducked my head into the smoke and ran through the library, bare feet over broken glass, and outside. I turned to see Roy dangling from a first-floor window and drop eight metres into the flowerbed, half stand, cry out with pain, collapse on the ground. Oddsocks was nowhere to be seen. The dog repeatedly came to the window too scared to jump until its tail on fire at last it leapt spinning with fright in the air hitting the ground with a squeal of injury.

The sound of my movement (even with the rattly leg iron clasped to me) was immense: breathing laboured, feet noisy on the gravel. But already crashes and the sound of timbers falling and the vigorous splintering sounds of the fire dominated all. I brushed the nail by chance against my moving thigh and pain surged, lifting me foolishly up on my insteps. Then I ran clear of the house over grass towards pines, out and away across to the lake's shore.

The water was black and flat calm. I got out on the wooden pier, could feel the planks flexing under my feet. I knelt down and touched cool water but there was no boat tied. Back on the bank I just made out the outline of the aluminium boat against the glowing house. Laid next to it was a body.

I felt Hagar's hair, still warm, tears in my eyes.

'Get off, will you!'

She sat up and stared at me, her eyes catching the light of the fire.

'About time,' she whispered, 'I fell asleep waiting.'

I handed over the iron caliper.

'I've been doing without it. I can, after all.'

'They threw it down to me, to scare me.'

'Let's get the boat. I brought the oars earlier.'

'How did you know?'

'I didn't. I planned on escaping myself today, that's all. I sent you the messages.'

'2 a.m. Exactly. How did you know I had a clock?'

'Didn't you?'

'Did they mistreat you?'

She said nothing. Then she said, 'I fed the dog potato leaves every chance I could. It was a strong dog. It was never sick.'

We heaved the boat over the black grass and onto the lake beach. It thundered over the sand and gravel. I thought I saw a figure running, or heard one. But swiftly we were on the dark water. Hagar rowed – I could not, my finger was still stuck with the nail – I would only remove it when I had a clean bandage to plug the hole.

The End

The end? That could not possibly be the end. I threw down the manuscript, stared at it, and then gathered it up contritely. More to the point, I knew now what to do. Time to implement something. Engage.

The next free day I had I drove across the city and staked out Bradawl's building. I parked, filled the meter with pound coins and without allowing one thought to distract me walked as if in seven-league boots to the tasteless glass entrance. I had lost interest in Cheryl's petty affairs, such as they might be; this was a test of something much, much, much, more important.

My disguise was no disguise. That was important. My clothes were merely City neutral: grey trousers, boring tie, dull light blue Gore-Tex jacket with a suit jacket poking out the bottom. Clerk's kit.

Up the slippery wide low steps I went, two at a time, sharp shiny Oxford shoes, rubber-soled though, for grip. I swung through the swing door and divided a small crowd as I approached the monster commanding the desk that guarded all access to the lifts. No electronic gates, no security tags, pre-9/11 human screening only.

I did not catch the eye of anyone nor did I stare; instead, I registered only barely the capped commissionaire and the pointy-chinned, red-lipped receptionist with her big book and several phones. Nor did I wait, instead I breezed, projecting one thought only: I am Dick Bradawl. I am Dick Bradawl. Not that I looked in the slightest bit like him. Not that I allowed myself to think this thought. As I strode I felt something was awry, something should be changed and in a stroke of genius my stride altered and my centre lowered – I had just put a bolt through my beam end and everybody knew it. Or rather they sensed it psychologically, the defining trait, boltdom, of silly Dick.

I was through but only just – at the last minute the secretary turned but then the sandwich man arrived with his tray of wares and blocked her view. We rode the lift together in silence to the floor occupied by Bradawl's boutique bank.

The lift door opened and I was unprepared for what I saw – nothing. A blank corridor of shut doors, veneered in micron-thin walnut all a bit bigger than those of normal size, the ceiling intimately low, the carpet thick. At one end a humungous window looked out over empty space and, in the distance, St Paul's Cathedral. Nice view.

I walked past each door. Inexplicably some had pairs of shiny shoes outside. One had two pairs. At the end of the corridor, where it bent to circumnavigate the outside of the building, I saw why. A bootblack, who looked like he had a PhD, wearing a bright-yellow jumpsuit, was polishing madly at a pair of brogues. He smiled, he had round glasses and thin blond hair, just like me. I smiled, too, losing for a second my all-conquering Dickness. The bootblack and me – overlooked by life, shafted bigtime by our lack of push and thrust.

Forget that. The next door was open. And the next. An empty office hung with Cheryl's signature prints, images of huge metal skeletal figures printed on handmade paper that draped like a roller blind to the floor. Not really an installation, more a small exhibition. I turned and saw, all at once, the sandwich man, Dick Bradawl's beaming burnished face and Cheryl at his elbow. If I was not Dick, who was I now? I tried the second trick, shrank myself to a dot and this time I did not care what the result was – a pure experiment. No greed or fear.

I was a dot and they walked past and did not see me. There was the proof, or at least enough to be going on with. Without a moment to lose I bought two smoothies from the sandwich man and headed back down the corridor. Outside one office I recognized the footwear. Into one exquisitely handcrafted Berlutti shoe went the peach and strawberry, into the other, chocolate and banana. They filled up nicely and I was off.

Another bit of proof: the receptionist called after me but I was too fast and she gave up. I was being me and she saw me.

Part Three

Hertwig

1

I telephoned Helmut.

'Ya,' he answered. In the background I could hear music and telltale sound effects, cash registers and a snatch of lyric. It went quiet. He, or Claudia, had turned it down.

'Ya,' Helmut said.

I told him I had read all the letters and papers, including Hertwig's handwritten manuscript.

'Yeah,' he switched to his English accent, 'I read it also many years ago but I've pretty much forgotten it now.'

This happens quite often. You find something mind-bendingly life-changing and someone else barely notices it. We talked about Hertwig, his amazing or forgettable life depending on your perspective.

'Really,' Helmut kept saying as I reminded him of things, 'Old Uncle did that?' I said I thought it might be worth publishing.

'You know, he was always planning to write a kind of sequel but I don't think he ever will.'

'Will?'

'Well, why not, he's old but he has all his abilities still.'

'But you told me he was dead.'

'No, I would never say that. Uncle Hertwig is, unless I am mistaken, living in Cairo still. Very alive, I think. He telephones twice each year.'

I did not ponder why Helmut had hidden Hertwig from me. I was certain that previously he had told me Hertwig was dead.

'You want his phone number?' said Helmut. It was that easy.

Except it wasn't. I kept putting off calling. I practised a few opening sentences but they rang false. And I didn't really know what to say after the opening sentences. I told myself I had never been that good on the phone, never really 'myself'. I tortured myself a bit more by remembering Cheryl was one of the few people I felt I could talk to with complete freedom, but not now. I'd given up driving by and dropping round. Meet the Dick. No thanks. From friends I heard that Richard Bradawl had been promoted yet again and with his colossal bonus had bought a ruined chateau together with an entire hamlet in the Pyrenees. No doubt he and Cheryl could retire there at the ripe old age of thirty-three and she could turn it into a sculpture village. Maybe they planned to live overseas permanently because I also heard she was looking for a job abroad. Perhaps in Paris or Monte Carlo, I mused with unimaginative bitterness.

Several weeks went by and though I thought about phoning Hertwig as if I really might phone I never did. Then, as if destiny was drawing me reluctantly on, I heard from my agent that there was the possibility of a paid trip to Egypt. Ozman Communications wanted me to attend a private tête-à-tête with Dr Ozman, one of Egypt's wealthiest men, lucky owner of the 3G licences not just for Egypt but large parts of Europe too. A showy, much-interviewed man, he wanted a company history even though his company was less than half a century old. Already money was being discussed, which is often a bad sign, but not always. I agreed to fly to Cairo.

The first thing I did after landing and ending up in the Berlin

Hotel (which the *Lonely Planet* recommended as '1930s', and which was also endorsed by Michael Palin, whose firmly cheerful visage shone out from several photos adorning the threadbare lobby), was to put a phone call through (you had to do this at the Berlin through the reception desk which had a Bakelite junction box as big as an ancient wireless full of jackplug sockets for each room) to Hertwig. I knew that fate, or something, had conspired to bring me to Egypt to meet him.

The phone rang. I let it ring for ages. No answer.

I went outside and engaged the streets, which were full of people sitting on round-backed chairs drinking glasses of tea and watching the traffic. There weren't nearly as many beggars as I'd thought and everyone had time for me. I went to the pyramids and got scammed out of a fiver for a 'special chance' to see a 'new tomb recently uncovered'. I almost didn't mind, telling myself I should accept such things in Egypt, but it did make me more cautious. I thought of Hertwig buying his little knife. Things hadn't changed. In fact my nervousness soon got the better of me and after a few half-hearted attempts to find out how to get to the Italian bunker I more or less gave up. I rang Hertwig's number again. No answer.

Ordinary people had time for me but not billionaires. Every time I was due to visit Dr Ozman I was told at the last minute he was elsewhere, busy or – my favourite – attending the opening of a new ice-cream parlour. He adored ice cream, everyone said. Later I found out it was a chain owned by him, but still.

There was still no answer from Hertwig, though finally Dr Ozman was free. His corporation lurked in a gigantic crenellated structure thirty storeys high, adorned with the words OZMAN COMMUNICATION. Lifts (I got in the wrong one at first) with carpeted walls shot me into the stratosphere. I was ushered into his office by a high-heeled-but-bent-over-from-carrying-too-many-heavy-files-but-still-beautiful secretary; it was a place of ceiling-to-floor tinted glass ('Great Nile view,' I said several times, meaning it), wall-to-wall leather sofas and modern art of a kind that was neither modern nor art. Dr Ozman was surprisingly neat, a careful ebullient man with teeth like cultured pearls, tinted in some curious way or perhaps it was the lighting up there in the penthouse, nearer to the sun. He had tiny hands and tiny fingers that tapered like speciality sausages.

'It is your first time in Egypt?' said Dr Ozman smiling, genuinely I felt. I agreed it was my first time though I had wanted to visit for ages. After these niceties Dr Ozman outlined in vague detail what he expected of a company history. It was as if the content of what he was saying was just being ad-libbed on the hoof and didn't really matter. I agreed to do the job though I suspected it might not happen – in the past I have been told the contract is in the post and then been let down. I'd believe it when I'd been paid.

With this business over I was really about to leave and get on the first plane back when something about Dr Ozman, the way he seemed open to suggestion in a way that corporate bosses usually are not, made me venture: 'By the way' – enunciated from the soft furnishing I was having some difficulty getting up from – 'do you know a German . . . academic, Dr Hertwig, Dr Martin Hertwig, by any chance?'

'Of course,' Ozman looked at his wristwatch that glittered with wealth, 'he will be opening his own exhibition of photographs in about one hour or one hour and a half. He is also a restorer of Islamic houses.'

The science of coincidences. Ozman had been invited but had more pressing business elsewhere, where, he did not say because when you have your own tower block with penthouse office overlooking the Nile you do not have to explain yourself very often to anyone. You lose the habit.

I gleaned from him the directions to Hertwig's retrospective, not far away in Garden City, a place name I recalled from his story. 'Good luck!' Ozman waved as the thick machined-metal and carpeted doors of the lift closed him out.

2

The gallery was in an old villa but the reception for the private view was on a large roof terrace which was strung with large fairy lights. There were walls for the photographs, but no ceilings. A warm night, a good night for not having anything between you and the firmament. I explained myself to a stubbly young Egyptian holding leaflets in English. He led me through a mixed crowd of foreigners and Egyptians with the slick well-showered look of wealth even if they had acne, which some of the boys and girls did I couldn't help noticing. I spotted Hertwig immediately – he was short and stout, buttoned up in a grey suit. He had half-round gold glasses for reading and he was signing copies of his book of photographs while standing. He didn't look eighty though I knew he had to be ninety. There was a huffing and puffing as he talked and a pronounced American accent.

'Dr Hertwig?'

'Huh? Not me, I'm afraid. That's Hertwig over there.'

'I'm sorry. Who are you?'

'The author.' He raised his eyebrows, not entirely pleased by my interruption, and then swivelled them in the direction of a man sitting in a deckchair (the seating was in deckchairs arranged higgledy-piggledy over the roof terrace). Hertwig was in white trousers and the most outrageous Hawaiian shirt I'd ever seen.

I approached more carefully this time. 'Er, Dr Hertwig?'

'Yes?' He was old but tanned with very white fluffy hair on the very top of his head and I couldn't help thinking of Stan Laurel, just for a moment. His eyes were large and light blue, sympathetic but not necessarily kindly.

'I thought this was your show?' I said.

'Not at all. George is a friend. Though I think I might be in one or two of his photographs. By the way have you seen them, they really are tremendous.' He had a delightful vagueness and a ringing clarity. I noticed he was wearing a very expensive Audemars Piaget wristwatch.

'Do you like my watch?' he whispered conspiratorially. 'It's a fake. I bought it this afternoon.'

I found that it was he who asked me the questions. After I spoke about his memoir (intending it as a lead into talking about his experiences) he adroitly turned the conversation and got me talking at length about the state of publishing today, him holding the cigarette I offered, then returning it as if he had really considered smoking it, though I noticed he had still not lit the cigar in his shirt pocket. 'I know, despite your kind comments, my style is so old fashioned. No, it is. Recently I have been reading young French and English authors to try and sound more modern. Georges Perec, Michel Houellebecq – I even attempted to write like your Martin – Martin Amis – but I couldn't.' He said it sadly as if he had really tried hard. Was he taking the piss? I told him Perec was dead and Martin Amis was pushing fifty if not fifty-five. 'Oh, still a young man, then,' said Hertwig wilfully misunderstanding me. What surprised, though, was the way he treated my reading of his memoirs and letters as a merely literary event. He gave the impression, and probably thought it too, that what he had written was just another piece of writing.

It did not seem right to become too intensely inquisitive with this light-hearted man but I did ask him about his father's aluminium teeth. He paused and then smiled. 'I suppose he did, but we were so used to them they made no impression. Anyway people in those days all kept their mouths closed. Who knows what horrors they were hiding!'

'But what about when he died? Was he buried in them?'

'My goodness, you *have* read my book, haven't you.'

I nodded.

'I think he got proper ones a few years before he died. And don't ask me whether the aluminium ones are still in some bank vault in Geneva or somewhere!'

'And what happened to Kasparius?'

Hertwig frowned. 'He died very shortly after being released by the Russians. They held him for ten years after the war – Siberia – a uranium mine, I believe. All *his* teeth fell out from radiation poisoning, I heard. Very unlucky really – all that silliness looking for antiquities for Himmler.'

Then, by a hand, or even finger gesture, he altered the whole tenor of the conversation, turning the spotlight on me but in a different way than before. I felt it was important that I ask him for advice – and what was uppermost on my mind was my fear of travelling alone in Egypt.

He turned his light blue eyes on me, eyes I later discovered were nearly blind from macular disease, and in a casual throw-away voice told me, 'On every journey there comes a point when you *have* to trust. You look for proof, evidence, recommendations but there are none – and you just have to trust.'

Then the bald, tall, polite but almost entirely bland figure of the German ambassador approached and in tones both loud and condescending praised Hertwig's many achievements, in, it appeared, the field of restoring old Islamic townhouses. The old man instantly turned on a stream of talk, friendly talk empty except for its ritual value, suddenly playing the role expected of him.

'We'll speak later,' he said in a theatrical whisper, 'about the really mystical information.' I hadn't even asked him about Hagar.

3

Nothing had changed except my mind. I took a train to Alexandria and a bus to El Alamein. From there, after a short ride in a microbus using directions gleaned from a much-folded photocopy of the *After the Battle* article, I found myself next to a line of telegraph poles on a dirt road in the desert. A rare pick-up stopped and turned. Two men at the front, villainous and laughing, all bad teeth and headscarves, said they'd take me anywhere: this through signs and their one word of English. 'Go'. I was all for waving them away and stopping another bus back to the city when I understood: this was that situation. I just had to trust.

So I did. They took me to the bunker, which was magnificent as bunkers go (made of huge squat concrete, its top in line with the level sands; there was a great hole in the corner which revealed a tangle of metal matrix and cast light onto a ghostly scene of broken bedsteads half buried in drifting sand) and well worth the visit (I chanced on a disembowelled BMW motorbike too) and yet I also knew I would probably be not visiting many more bunkers in the future.

4

I called Hertwig when I got back to Cairo at the new number he had given me (he had recently moved, which explained my earlier unsuccessful attempts to contact him). It was as if he had been expecting my call, though by some conversational sleight of hand he made it impossible for me to relate *his* effect on my journey to the bunker. It was as if he had misheard me and I suspected he might be slightly deaf. Then he made a friendly show of getting it into his head that I would be able to edit his book into something publishable. 'Let's meet up and talk,' he said eagerly.

I met him a day later at his hotel, in rooms almost totally devoid of character. 'I hate it here,' he said, waving his fleshy pink hand at the yellow chintz curtains, made brighter yellow by the setting sun. 'Too much noise, don't you think?' There was, it was true, an excess of honking and revving from the street below but I had assumed Cairo was all like that.

'Not at all, I have a friend who may let me her villa in Sakkara. Terrible mosquitoes but so quiet! You've caught me between apartments, I'm afraid.'

On the glass-topped oval dining table was a mahogany, I guessed, writing box. Mid-nineteenth century with a lovely carved top inlaid with some Arabic script shaped to look like a ship with a sail. This box was the start of something weird. Very weird.

'Ah, the box,' said Hertwig.

'It's nice.'

'It's a campaign desk, I understand it once belonged to a Turkish general who, it is said, gave it to Dr Ragab.'

I looked with real admiration at the box. I opened it to view the emerald-leather writing surface, which when lifted revealed a host of nested drawers and cubbyholes. I could not help but imagine Dr Ragab writing things, probably with a quill pen, on that very box. I looked up to see the lovely smile of Hertwig. Benign, playful yet objective, distanced somehow. I was gripped by the most atavistic of urges, the primitive belief in religious remains, magic objects, totems. But how could I be sure? It all came back to that, it always did.

'I have been told by a friend who used to work for Sotheby's that such a box is worth at a minimum a thousand sterling.' Hertwig may have been a nonagenarian scholar and house-restorer, he was also a consummate salesman employing a phoney objective value to make his price stick. I didn't mind. I wanted to pay, almost the more the better.

'How about twelve hundred?' I suggested. 'I would hate that you would feel short-changed.'

Hertwig gave an apologetic yet expansive look that both conveyed his concern that I should think I had to overpay and yet also did not distract away from the business at hand which was to sell.

'I think a thousand would be fine,' he said, 'what do you think?'

'I think it would be fine too.'

But when I got the box back to my hotel room at the Berlin, I noticed it was scuffed and chipped in places and one of the interior drawers was missing which I thought probably meant it was worth less. I had gleaned at the photo-exhibition that Hertwig was not well off and I suspected he really needed the £1,000 I had just given him in fifty-pound notes (convenient hotel-owning friend of his who took it off my card no commission) but the inevitable reaction set in and I felt conned. I looked at the admittedly beautiful portable writing desk: so what if it belonged to Dr Ragab?

I gazed at the box and on several occasions examined it closely for hinged panels, secret messages, keys, gems or any other esoteric ephemera. All I found was a stippled rubber 'finger' for counting money and two paperclips. I sighted the box up to see if it had a false bottom. It did not. Gradually it dawned on me that this box was the antidote to all my silly imaginings about Hertwig. And yet it revealed he had something more valuable to offer.

I was aware of the tradition of making students pay for esoteric knowledge that is assumed by the ignorant to be always 'free'. As Ragab told Hertwig – 'no knowledge worth having is ever free'. I knew the theory but now I had the experience. I had stupidly thought buying an object owned by a 'Master' would magically have some transformative effect on me. I knew that was just wishful thinking. I had known it before, but only in words, now I knew it for real. The second lesson.

5

Back in Ealing I set my box on the window sill and watched it raining outside. Cheryl had left several messages in her chirpy way, her attempts at being wacky simply tedious at times, a kind of wan substitute for energy and humour. As always I put off calling back.

Everyone who visited the flat commented on the quality of the box and the obvious workmanship.

Then the phone rang on my round table in front of the drizzly window.

'It's Ozman here, yes, yes, I thought you should know, poor Hertwig has fallen, twice in fact, broke his hip and his rib and now there is some awful gastric complication. I thought you should know.'

I was touched that such a leader of industry and world-renowned businessman as Dr Ozman should take the time to let me know about Hertwig. But then again I had always suspected, in more fanciful moments, that he, too, owed his success to something gleaned from Ragab's teaching. And though he had never mentioned it, as such, he nodded as if to say, of course, when I spoke, of Hertwig's apprenticeship so many years ago.

I decided to fly immediately. Concern mingled with selfishness. I wanted my fill of 'wisdom' before he died. Then I dismissed this idea as nonsense and recalled the box. On the plane I sucked boiled sweets and looked out of the window at the wavering metal wings, so sharply clear against the horizon.

6

It was late at night when I landed. That old Cairo smell hit me, the rich fug of car exhaust and all the spices of the Orient. I took a taxi to an address scribbled on a Rizla paper (old one, I'd given up smoking for some reason I couldn't fathom). Hertwig's new apartment was in Garden City. He was at last out of hospital. I took the wooden-doored elevator up to the sixth floor and knocked on number 14. There was some fumbling with the locks and I was shocked by his appearance, shocked because he looked both much older and yet younger too. His white hair had thinned to a nothing of greasy swirls on his head. The tan had greyed but his eyes were more intensely alive and his jawline sharpened, there was a vigour about him I had never noticed before. He wore a grey silk suit that caught the moonlight.

'It's awful in here,' was the first thing he said, 'let's go somewhere else.'

'How are you?'

'Well, apart from the hair, which I think may just grow back. I met someone who ate nothing but vitamin B tablets, turned his urine orange but his hair grew back. Worth a try.'

'Yes, definitely.'

'Awful hospital. Useless, in fact. The old German hospital in Bab El Luk. Stupid to think of going there. I should have flown home. My God – those Egyptian doctors! They left a swab inside me the size of a Kleenex box. That was the problem as I told you – after my appendix burst they left that in me and I was . . . rather sick, as you might imagine. No sticks, though. I've been training myself.'

Without even a limp, or a very well-disguised one, Hertwig descended the steps outside the building and into the waiting cab. Getting into the front seat he misjudged the distance and sat down with a hard bump. His face creased with pain but he wiped it away almost instantly. He spoke in rapid Arabic, '*Naredy Italiano, Qasr El Nil.*'

He turned heavily on the seat. 'The Italian club, I've heard they have just got some new wines in. Though I will only drink a glass – even that is forbidden but it makes me feel so much better.'

Hertwig talked and heard what I said, gone now all trace of the earlier deafness and the earlier vagueness, affectations that served him well in more leisured times, now his jawline was set more firmly, more youthfully, eyes shining with purpose, vigour it seemed to me coming from heaven knows where. The story of his botched operation, the fall down the steps of the American University bookshop, the second fall while answering the door to the doctor visiting about the first fall, the swollen and threatening appendix and the recovery of the lost swab – all this sounded enough to kill anyone and yet it had made Hertwig younger, in a way, in a way that was understandable to anyone who met him. That hair loss, which was so shocking at first sight, images of chemo, death masks, etc. on closer inspection, which I now made every few minutes, only served to emphasize the purposeful vitality of his features.

The taxi man drove us into the gated compound of the Italian

Club. 'You've never been?' said Hertwig joyfully. 'It is the best-kept secret of this town. I have been a regular since 1931.'

I had in my mind all the questions I had as yet been unable to ask. If I did not now I might never get an answer, it might be too late. Hertwig picked this thought up effortlessly as he studied the menu. 'I aim to be around for a good while yet.' I believed him.

'Did you ever see the hermit again? The Russian hermit?'

'Oh him – poor fellow, the British picked him just before they left – late 1951 – only a few months before the end of his "contract". Ionides refused to pay. The poor chap finally settled in Cyprus to work as a mechanic. Must be dead now.'

'When did Dr Ragab die exactly?' I asked.

'The same year 1951, yes, then.'

'How old was he?'

'Not that old, perhaps seventy-six or so. He was killed by mistake, you know.'

'I didn't know.'

'He was walking from his apartment in Garden City, where he lived at that time during the week, and an enraged *zebaleen*, a rubbish collector, attacked him with a single bicycle spoke. He was stabbed through the neck and chest and died a day later. Then it transpired the madman who killed him had mistaken him for some fellow in another apartment who owed him money.'

'Couldn't he have . . .'

'Saved himself with all his wisdom etc.? Yes, that does tend to cross one's mind, doesn't it? But I rather think he knew his time was up. He'd done his work, you see. Time to move on.'

'What was his work?'

'Some of it you know from reading my book. The rest was

largely hidden. He had a great deal of influence. I happen to believe the relative restraint of Nasser's takeover was partly his doing.'

'But wasn't he dead by then?'

'He sowed seeds, if you recall.'

There was a longish gap while we savoured our food. I started up again. 'About the Universal Language . . .'

Hertwig held up his hand. 'Look,' he pointed, 'a hoopoe. In that tree.' I swivelled round to catch a glimpse of the legendary, though not uncommon, bird with its fan of head feathers. When I turned back Hertwig was sitting watching me. I would not be put off.

'About the . . .'

'Yes, well you see, that was then. Even when I wrote that manuscript it was intended only for my nieces and nephews, I knew that it could so easily create . . . the wrong impression.'

'How do you mean?'

'Things that have a developmental value must change with the times and the place in which they happen. The old style of teaching doesn't really work today, it was designed for a different age when tradition had schooled people in unthinking obedience. We could work with that, at least Ragab could. Part of the trouble I had was adapting to that requirement of obedience. Of course the aim is still the same, to free the student, if that is what you want to call him, or her, from the controlling whims of the outer self. Now it might be more appropriate to use hints, suggestions, outwit the outer self by superficially involving him, certainly not provoking his resistance. You could try otherwise but I imagine you'd end up with a cult.'

Hertwig smiled. 'The pasta here is surprisingly good, as is

the *bruschetta toscana*, Italian expatriates come here specially to eat it.'

'What happened after you escaped? I know you told me broadly that you came here with Hagar, but how did you manage it?'

'With a great deal of luck, I might say! I told you Hagar died in 1978 or thereabouts, I'm no good with dates. We'd separated by then, amicable, as you might imagine. She had become very interested in the Arctic tern of all things, a migratory bird of vast ambition, as you probably know better than I, she took to painting them and following the things everywhere – from the frozen north down through Nunavuk across to the Caribbean and then to the lonely rock of Tristan de Cunha, South Shetland and so on. Wrapping the globe in a sympathetic migration all of her own, you might say. She told me that she had come to believe that you had to squeeze everything you could from a relationship and then move on, migrate so to speak.' He smiled at the thought of it. 'A tough way of looking at things,' he added.

'How did you feel?'

'A little sad. But she was right, besides we got on much better after she had left on her journeys and I certainly wasn't going down to the Southern Oceans, no thank you. Egypt has the perfect climate, even in the heat of summer the breezes are magnificent, divinely inspired.'

'Earlier, though, what happened? Where the manuscript ended?'

'Where did it end?'

It seemed an odd question.

'When you and Hagar finally got away from the ex-prisoners.'

'Ah – those *fucking* convicts!'

He showed me his hand, the index finger with a tiny thickened nail and lined with a spider scar of raised white flesh.

'Dr Ragab told me later that it was a miracle that my methods actually worked.'

'A miracle?'

'In a manner of speaking. Anyway, we rowed away across that lake. On the other side we stated walking to the nearest village – miles away, I might add.

'Hagar had a carton of Lucky Strikes, stolen from our captors. They were the only currency at that time – and they bought us freedom: train tickets to Karlsruhe, where I knew my cousins were living.'

Hertwig looked up. 'We borrowed money – of course my family had been very clever at hiding their wealth away, almost certainly collaborated with the regime, at least through bribery – I know that for certain. That money, or a fraction of it, bought our escape, which was how we thought of it, to Egypt. Which was then, as now, rather in favour of disgraced Germans, Hitler being, until recently, not an unpopular boy's name.'

'I didn't know that,' I said.

'Oh yes – a prominent defence minister is called Mohamed Hitler Tautaw: but his speeches are rarely reported by the Deutsches Press Agency, I can assure you.'

It wasn't quite the story I had been expecting. It was just the externals. It didn't answer anything. Hertwig maybe sensed this and continued.

'My new studies with Dr Ragab took on a rather different form. Hagar was involved as well. Ragab had changed direction. He now spent much time starting and encouraging sporting clubs – football, handball, even boxing. He also founded a large publishing company devoted to children's literature. We helped with all that, especially with any international business. Though he had contacts among Nasser's group his villa and much of his property was confiscated in 1952 – after he had died. His relatives lost the property though acquired considerable wealth, in the form of valuable old Korans Ragab bought cheaply in his final years. Hundreds of them stored in especially dry conditions in Aswan. I believe they are worth even more now, millions no doubt, especially to oil-rich Emiratis. One of his nephews looks after that side of his legacy, the financial side. But I know very little else. You see, though I worked with him almost every day when he was in Cairo in those last years, he was always making trips. One never asked him where he was going. You just didn't.'

Hertwig mopped his brow with his napkin, though it was not a particularly hot evening and he was not sweating. 'I think that is about all I can say.'

'But Hagar . . . when you were in the bunker?'

'Ah, yes, always a mystery I'm afraid.'

'She never said?'

'Never.'

'Did they . . .'

'Perhaps. Or perhaps not. She only said, "Don't ask." So I thought about that for several years. I was tempted on many occasions but I didn't. And after five years of not asking I decided it was for the best and now it hardly seems important.'

The waiter appeared brandishing dessert menus on dog-eared plastic-coated card. 'Never very reassuring, this kind of menu, is it?' commented Hertwig. 'But usually the chocolate mousse or the coffee ice-cream is worth a try.'

Hagar kept secrets, Cheryl liked to tell all, almost all. I knew the time of her birth. How she lost her virginity. The occasion she interrupted sex to both throw up and suffer diarrhoea (food bug on a Greek island). I had driven with her past her old primary school in Haywards Heath, her secondary school (once grammar, now a comprehensive going downhill), her student hall in Manchester ('Madchester – it really was'). I'd met her living relatives and felt I knew most of her dead ones. Cheryl told all and I listened. I don't like secrets, really, except my own.

Hertwig by now ought to have been tired, but was not. As the candles in Chianti bottles waxed elaborate filigree buttresses he was summoning more energy from somewhere, a focusing. The night air seemed thicker with the wine drunk. I noticed how little he had eaten, worked-over food was still on his plate.

He seemed to be gathering himself. And at a gesture I understood was a summoning, but subtle and not at all overbearing I leaned forward. He spoke assuredly, almost as if reading off something inside his head.

'The language of enlightenment is constantly being appropriated. The Universal Language was Ragab's way around that, but that, too, has had its time. Too much system. We're living in a time where truth, as expressed, resides almost wholly in the informal, the unofficial, in surprising places, in practices not lengthy dissertations. On a different level the reverence for the entrepreneur in every modern culture reflects this inner conviction – that they at least know something real. Something about human nature and something about the world. Something most specialists have sadly lost.'

He paused for what seemed like a precise period and continued.

'One generation finds the religious sentiments of the previous generation cracked and hollow – why? Because the genuine has already been appropriated and used in the service of amusement, excitement and a sense of importance. It's even happening now. Many modern 'spiritual' writers, some of whom, you have mentioned, are spread far and very, very thin. They may or may not have developmental value. What does happen is their words are used like tokens by those who see them only as yet more words. Clever people are very good at pretending to have understood, or deploying the right tokens and avoiding useful experience.'

I knew better than to ask the next question: 'So how do you know?' He knew, that, at least, I knew.

I had early on decided to limit the advice I sought from Hertwig (I almost wrote Dr Ragab then). Most advice is ignored. If I asked advice I wanted it to be sincere, that I would follow it. For this reason I never asked his advice about the trivial matter of Cheryl and me.

That night, as I dropped him off in the taxi – he sat down slower this time with much more grace – he was already learning how to deal with his ailment (if I glimpsed anything about Hertwig it was not any especial brilliance, rather an ability to adapt without losing anything of himself) anyway, that night I formed a plan.

The bunker (in Ealing) would be sold. I would move to Egypt and study with Hertwig (i.e. spend time with him, perhaps in editing his MS). Almost as soon as I made this decision and contacted an estate agent and started showing young professional couples around (the steel door went down very well), I received a call from Dr Ozman. 'I hear that Hertwig is a little better, that is good. By the way, I have authorized the first payment for our history. I am sure you will do a good job of it.'

Though I had saved a goodly portion of my 'aluminium'

money, enough to live on in Cairo for many months, I now had an alibi, the only kind you can't argue with these days – going where the work is. Some kind of turning point in my luck had been reached, I could feel it almost palpably, a growing confidence, a relaxation of anxieties. I didn't even worry when I forgot to renew my subscription to *After the Battle*.

7

Selling my flat was time-consuming but not so very difficult. Owing to the distorted property market I stood to make a sizeable profit, which I quickly got used to. I even started devising ways to spend it. Once I got to Cairo.

I spoke to Hertwig quite often by telephone. He was getting email set up, he said, it was just happening in Cairo – this was a few years ago, I might add. He was getting better. 'I think I've gained some healing energy from our last meeting,' he said.

As people approach death they either become more light-filled or more dark-filled. Maybe they become more themselves but I'm not sure. Maybe they are so filled with pain-killing drugs they cannot communicate. I had seen a few people just before they died, usually of a variant of cancer, and it was not a pleasant thing at all. I have seen people dying of brain tumours completely at peace with the world. Maybe the pain is more important than we think. Most people do not fear death they fear the pain of dying. Maybe we need to learn how to deal with pain while we can.

I made one more trip to Cairo to find an apartment to rent. When I met Hertwig I knew he was dying. He had a strained look about him, and he ate and drank nothing in my company, yet his eyes showed a decision, it was just a decision I felt, to not give up and this caused an immense upwelling of energy. I could almost feel it crackling off him. This was my miracle if I needed it.

Cheryl phoned me out of the blue. 'I've been busy,' she said, 'travelling a lot. I've a got a new job – teaching art therapy for Save the Children – in Egypt, in Cairo.' Somehow I was not surprised. The science of coincidence.

'But what about Richard?' I said. 'And his amazing metal dick?'

'Oh, *that*,' she said. 'He got promoted by his company – I mean, he sort of went a bit strange after that. I never really liked him, not that much, though he was funny. (Funny?) It was all a bit of a *performance*, I felt. How about you?'

I told her everything including the fact I had found a good-sized apartment off Qsar Al-Aini Street for only $200 a month.

She was coming to Egypt. I felt the doors opening, infinitely high and thick steel doors, bunker doors if ever there were, the light a wedge of growing brightness.

On our first night in Cairo I took Cheryl to the Italian Club. She said, 'All along I was waiting for something special to happen.'

'What sort of thing?'

'Something like this.'

'Why me?' I said.

'Oh, *you know*,' she said. Then she said something about me being a bit kinder. Which I took to mean less moneyed, less good looking, less.

'You remember putting up that sculpture in the rain for me?' Then I realized she meant that kind of kinder.

That night I lay awake thinking and staring into blackness; Cheryl's breathing, snuffling, awkward inhalation just audible. Oddly reassuring to think she was almost snoring.

I thought about Hagar, her luminosity, the Arctic terns. His life, her life, not mine nor that of anyone else. A new sort of learning could begin here. I had my miracle, no more waiting. The doors did not, after all, require infinite effort in their opening. Somehow, I sensed, I would have to get used to the extra light.

THE END

Robert Twigger
Cairo
May 2008